A BRIDGE OF STARS

A Shade of Vampire, Book 24

Bella Forrest

ALSO BY BELLA FORREST:

A SHADE OF VAMPIRE SERIES:

Derek & Sofia's story:

A Shade of Vampire (Book 1)

A Shade of Blood (Book 2)

A Castle of Sand (Book 3)

A Shadow of Light (Book 4)

A Blaze of Sun (Book 5)

A Gate of Night (Book 6)

A Break of Day (Book 7)

Rose & Caleb's story:

A Shade of Novak (Book 8)

A Bond of Blood (Book 9)

A Spell of Time (Book 10)

A Chase of Prey (Book 11)

A Shade of Doubt (Book 12)

A Turn of Tides (Book 13)

A Dawn of Strength (Book 14)

A Fall of Secrets (Book 15)

An End of Night (Book 16)

Ben & River's story:

A Wind of Change (Book 17)

A Trail of Echoes (Book 18)

A Soldier of Shadows (Book 19)

A Hero of Realms (Book 20)

A Vial of Life (Book 21)
A Fork Of Paths (Book 22)
A Flight of Souls (Book 23)

A SHADE OF DRAGON:

A Shade of Dragon 1
A Shade of Dragon 2
A Shade of Dragon 3

A SHADE OF KIEV TRILOGY:

A Shade of Kiev 1
A Shade of Kiev 2
A Shade of Kiev 3

BEAUTIFUL MONSTER DUOLOGY:

Beautiful Monster 1
Beautiful Monster 2

For an updated list of Bella's books,
please visit www.bellaforrest.net

Join my VIP email list and I'll personally send you an email
reminder as soon as my next book is out!
Click here to sign up: www.forrestbooks.com

Contents

BEN

I could hardly believe what we'd done. I had proposed and River had accepted. We were engaged. Even though, for all I knew, in less than three days I could be stripped of this body and returned to my previous half-existence.

If ever I'd needed an incentive to hold on to this physical form, I had it now.

Having River accept me the way she had, even though she was fully aware of how uncertain my future—our future—was, left me high. I shot up with her into the sky with abandon, barely paying attention to how high up we were or how fast I was flying.

I lost myself fully in her kiss until, finally, I came to my senses.

Time was ticking and we still had a terrifying number of obstacles ahead of us. If we did not leave now, we were making our chances of success even slimmer.

Pausing in our ascent, I began drifting us back downward, all the while making the most of these last moments we had alone together. I had no way of knowing how long it would be before we would find private time again. We continued kissing and caressing until our feet hit the island's boundary. Unlocking our lips, I guided her to climb onto my back so that she would be in a more secure position.

"Corrine!" we both began to yell. "Ibrahim! Shayla!"

Then I called out to my parents while River did the same. We shouted out any name and made as much noise as possible, even as I roamed with her over the surface of the barrier.

"Coming!" a voice finally called up. Corinne's voice.

And then I heard another voice.

"Benjamin?"

To my confusion, it did not come from beneath us, but rather from behind. I whirled around with River to find myself face to face with...

"Aisha?" River and I gasped in unison.

The young jinni hovered several feet away from us. She looked worse for wear. The smoke that surrounded the lower half of her body appeared duller and thinner than usual, and her skin was less radiant, almost gray. Her face looked tired and worn.

"What are you doing here?" I gaped.

"What are *you* doing here?" she asked, staring at me as though I had come back from the dead. Her face twisted in confusion. "Benjamin, what are you?"

I barely registered her question and all curiosity I'd felt at the shock of seeing her at The Shade evaporated. Excitement coursed through me.

A jinni.

We've found a jinni!

Maybe destiny was finally turning a kind eye upon me. *About time...*

"I managed to evade the Elder by taking a potion Arron gave me." I gave her a rapid recap explaining how I ended up in the body of a fae. "But it's on loan," I said, getting to the crux of the matter. "I can keep it no longer than three days unless I bring the fae a jinni." Well, actually I had told Sherus I'd bring an army of jinn, but failing that, perhaps one would suffice.

Aisha's mouth dropped open. "You made a pact with a fae?"

"Yes," I said, impatient. "Aisha, I desperately need your help. I don't know exactly what the fae need the jinn to do, but you're powerful, aren't you?"

To my horror, her shoulders sagged. "Not any more."

"What?"

Aisha heaved a deep sigh and clasped one palm to her forehead, rubbing it wearily. "The Drizans took my family, just like I suspected. I still haven't recovered from the shock, let alone the grief. Mourning drains a jinni like a bloodsucker. I don't know when I'd be of any use to you again..."

My heart dropped to the pit of my stomach. I was about to ask Aisha whether she could just try — at least hear what Sherus' task was — but then I realized that was the stupidest idea imaginable. The risk was far too great. If she really couldn't help Sherus, then I would have returned to the fae not only without the promised army, but also incapable of fulfilling their demands. I was sure he'd swipe my body from me in an instant, and likely, in his rage, even take me back to The Underworld. A place I could safely say I would not want to visit again.

No. I had to get over the disappointment of Aisha not having her powers, or at least claiming to not have them. We were back to the original plan. We had to free the Nasiris from the Drizans.

Corrine emerged through the boundary muttering, "Sorry for the delay..." Her voice trailed off as she laid eyes on

Aisha.

"Aisha Nasiri is with me," I said quickly, "You should know by now that the Nasiris are ally rather than foe." A notion I understood was hard to accept for Corrine after the Nasiris had turned her into a dove.

Aisha barely spared a glance for Corrine—or River, for that matter—her focus on me.

"Come down with us," I said to the jinni. "Somehow, we need to save your family."

The look the jinni gave me made my stomach sink to new depths. "I don't think that's even possible."

But I blocked out her words. I couldn't believe them. I wouldn't believe them.

The Nasiris were the key to this body. The key to my future with River. And, dammit, I was going to pry every one of that family from the Drizans' hands... even if it was the last thing I did.

Lucas

As strange as this reunion was for my younger brother, it was tenfold stranger for me.

Hell, I was still getting used to the feel of soil beneath my feet, the wind blowing against my skin, the sounds of the living world—so many sounds that I had forgotten even existed. Now that I had been deprived of it all for decades, I sensed it all in far greater detail than I would have even as a vampire. The sensations surrounding me were enough to bring me to my knees, but then to be faced so suddenly with my brother, my sister... my son... My mind struggled to hold it all in.

A myriad of emotions had overwhelmed me on seeing

Jeramiah leap out of that boat… on him seeing me for the first time in his life. He was a grown man now, but I had spied on him enough times as a boy to recognize his features.

All the bitterness, the resentment, self-hatred and regret that the ghouls had given me ample opportunity to harbor over the years roared to the surface. The regret for having abandoned him, for having willingly given up one of the truest pleasures life had to offer a man—raising a son—erupted like a seething boil. Every part of me ached, mind, body and soul.

But at least whatever happened to me next—even if this body was swiped away from me in a few days and I was thrust into the ghouls' Necropolis—I'd met my son. And I had said that I was sorry. And I'd told him the truth that his mother had been too kind to tell him.

That I was a coward.

A waste of space.

Indeed, now it felt like my whole life had been a waste of space. I'd been so concerned with the life I'd thought I should be living as ruler of The Shade—obviously superior to Derek—that I'd forgotten to live the life that I had been gifted. And it was, indeed, a gift. Any creature with a beating heart possessed the greatest gift the universe had to offer. *A gift to be guarded, treasured, and appreciated every damn day.*

And when it had been taken away from me so suddenly…

so unexpectedly...

I still remembered the night I'd exhaled my last breath. The last moments of my former life during the battle in The Oasis. I'd had Sofia in my grasp. And I had been so sure that I would finally pry her forever from my brother. But that envy had made me blind. Blind to the hunter aiming a gun at me. Blind to him pulling the trigger. That envy had made me blind my whole life.

Everything had been taken from me in a flash. And all the things that had formerly been invisible to me about my life had sprung into existence in vivid detail. Only then, I could not touch any of it.

A month spent in The Underworld would've been enough to make me cast aside my jealousy and determine to live the rest of my life in its own full, perfect glory. But... almost two decades? I was shocked that I'd even been conscious enough to utter a single word when Ben had found me in my pool, let alone form a sentence.

Now here I found myself, standing in a body again—a real body—relishing everything in sight... even the familiar sight of my younger brother, looking only a few years older than when I'd left him. Now that was a strange feeling.

It was bizarre to realize that I was hardly capable of feeling jealous of him anymore. Not even when I knew that he'd gotten Sofia for himself in the end. He'd even ruled over this place as king for the past two decades—a position I'd always considered my own—while I had been locked up in hell. How could I feel jealous of anything when my spirit soared so high? When my heart was beating, and I had my son standing just next to me. When I was back in The Shade. *Back home.*

After Derek had asked me what on earth happened to me, of course I was expecting the barrage of questions that followed. Even from my son, whom I had rendered quite speechless after my admission that I had not been a victim of circumstance, but rather a coward who had willingly abandoned him. I began to answer, still unable to shake the strangeness of talking to my brother. I tried to remember the last words I had exchanged with him, and I could not even recall them now. But whatever they were, I was certain they would not have been pleasant.

Sofia, Vivienne and Ben's twin sister uprooted from their spots by the jetty and hurried over. As Sofia arrived at Derek's side, I could not miss the way she clutched his arm. It took me back in time to when Sofia had first arrived in The Shade. When I interrupted their time together, she'd always flinch and move closer to Derek, as though I were a venomous snake. I doubted she was conscious of her instinctive action now, or how identical it was to when she had still been seventeen.

Vivienne broached the invisible barrier Derek had drawn for himself about four feet from me, and closed the distance between us. As she reached out a trembling hand to clutch my own, she was warm. She was human. Yet she couldn't have been one for long, because she didn't look any older than when I had last seen her.

My heart hammered as Vivienne wrapped her arms around me and pulled me in for a tight hug. *Vivienne. My sister. My darling younger sister.* As much as I could not deny that even seeing my younger brother's face had been a relief, my heart filled with true affection on seeing my sister. I slipped my own arms around her and hugged her back, just as strongly.

"I've missed you, Lucas," she whispered, and I felt her breath hitch.

"I... I've missed you too," I murmured, my throat tight.

As hard as she hugged me, her body also felt rigid in shock, as though her brain was still struggling to accept that this really was me. Her older brother. Lucas Dominic Novak. Back in The Shade. Back where I belonged.

I closed my eyes as she kissed my cheek, trying not to leak tears. I felt embarrassed enough as it was for my breakdown in front of Derek on greeting my son. But it was a vain attempt.

When I could hold off answering questions no longer, I

went on with my story. Truth be told, there wasn't all that much to tell anymore. The bulk of my days had been spent in The Underworld, shrouded in darkness, where I'd barely been aware of myself. But I told them everything I could remember: leaving my physical body in The Oasis, roaming The Shade for some time. Then moving on to where I'd thought that I was supposed to go, only to be caught by the fae and thrust into hell.

I paused, looking from one face to another, before averting my eyes to the ground. I found it difficult to hold eye contact for too long, especially with my brother. But I would've given anything to know what was going through his mind—heck, through all of their minds. Even despite Vivienne's affection, I still didn't know if I was welcome here. That had been why I was so hesitant to come to this island in the first place. I hadn't thought I could handle the stress of seeing my family again. But now that I was here, surrounded by them, I couldn't be more thankful that Ben had insisted I follow him. It was cathartic. And I realized that I needed this for my own sanity—to confront my past, no matter how uncomfortable it was.

Sofia cleared her throat, drawing my eyes to her beautiful green ones even despite myself. I found myself quickly exhausted as she eyed me intently, her gaze far stronger than mine.

Then, when she spoke, her voice sent tingles down my spine. I'd almost forgotten what her voice sounded like.

"All of us have learned to forgive on this island, Lucas," she said.

Derek's jaw tightened. Although he didn't say anything to the contrary, I couldn't help but sense he was less generous in his thinking than Sofia.

"If you've changed," Vivienne continued, looking up at me through her glistening violet-blue eyes, "I don't see why we wouldn't all welcome you back with open arms."

There was a span of silence as I considered how to respond, or maybe not to respond at all. I had changed, even against my own will; that much was undeniable. But it didn't feel like mere words sufficed in this situation.

Gulping, I nodded. Even though my words were in response to Vivienne, it was Derek whom I looked straight at as I replied, "I suppose you will be the judge of that."

Ben

Corrine, Aisha, River and I arrived at the Port to find Lucas and Jeramiah standing in the same position, but now with the rest of my family surrounding them: my father, mother, aunt and sister. Marcilla, Nolan and Chantel still hung some distance away, wandering around by the trees and gazing at our island in wonder.

I guessed from the looks on my family's faces that Lucas had explained to them what had happened, at least in part. That was good. It saved us time. Sensing us approach, they twisted around, eyes bulging as they spotted Aisha hovering next to me and River.

"This is Aisha," I addressed my parents. "One of the

Nasiris. In case Lucas hasn't mentioned, we have less than three days to present a gang of fae with an army of jinn, or these bodies will be stripped from us forever... and then there's no saying what will become of me. We need to retrieve the Nasiris from the Drizans so I can take them to the fae."

My mother tensed with fear. "The Drizans," she murmured.

"We must call an emergency meeting," my father said, never one to skip a beat, even as he still appeared to be in shock. "Corrine, would you fetch the rest of our Council?"

The witch nodded before vanishing.

Five minutes later, we were seated in the Great Dome, waiting for the rest of the Council to arrive. I couldn't help but catch a glimpse of Lucas as my mother and father took seats at the head of the table. I wished I could glimpse into his mind. Jeramiah sat next to Lucas, and I was still burning to know how he'd gotten here. I'd deliberately been avoiding meeting my cousin's gaze because I knew that I would only end up glaring at him. It would take me a long time to forgive Jeramiah "Stone" for what he'd done to my family.

River sat beside me, while Aisha perched on my other side. Nolan, Chantel and Marcilla had also come with us and they sat further up the table. We watched the door as, one by one, the new arrivals gaped at Lucas, looking as though they'd been winded. And when Claudia, one of the last to enter, entered with Yuri, her belly protruding beneath a light pink dress, she positively shrieked on laying eyes on her old flame. She stared at Lucas, wide-eyed and gasping.

Then her eyes shot toward my father, digging into him for an explanation. Derek merely shrugged, and gestured for her to sit down with the rest of us.

As if Claudia would do that. She turned on Lucas again, daring to move closer to him.

"Lucas?" she breathed, blinking rapidly as though she were attempting to wake up.

Lucas nodded, a grimace on his face. "It is I," he murmured.

Claudia clutched Yuri's arm for support. The blood drained from her face, and it looked like she was about to faint. "Oh, Lord..."

Yuri ushered her to a seat on the opposite end of the table.

"There will be time for questions later," my father said, as the last of our Council—Jeriad—entered.

From what I could see, the only member missing was Aiden, who would no doubt be overwhelmed in a teary reunion with Kailyn.

As the door snapped shut and Jeriad took his seat, my father began, "First, acknowledging the elephant in the room." He pointed toward Lucas and Jeramiah. "Yes, these men you see before you are indeed Lucas and his son Jeramiah."

Questions erupted but my father steamrolled over them. "We need to set our immediate attention on freeing the Nasiris from the Drizans." My father went on to explain our predicament and my promise to the fae. "There could be great danger involved," he went on, eyeing everyone sternly. "And even if all of you were willing, I think we should make this a party of no more than ten. What do you say, Aisha?" He turned on the teenage jinni. "You should tell us everything you know about the Drizans."

Aisha parted her dry lips, shoulders still sagging. "They're worse than animals," she murmured.

"Tell us about their lair," I urged. "Is it possible for us to penetrate it?"

"Not me," she replied in a strained voice. "I've been banished from The Dunes."

"What?" I asked.

"I've been banished. Kicked out. Expelled. There's no way that I can go anywhere near the Drizans' palace."

Oh, crap. And to think that I'd been so excited on seeing Aisha at first, even going to the extent of considering that she might be up to help us solo; now she was telling us she couldn't even set foot in the realm of the jinn.

"Jeriad." My father turned to the shifter. "It seems we will need to call upon your help once again in dealing with the Drizans."

Jeriad's eyes darkened. "Freeing the Nasiris is not something that we can request. Not after we just agreed to give them to the clan. I must also make clear, Derek, that although my people were on decent terms with the Drizans in the past, and they owed us a favor here and there, we're certainly not the best of friends. They might even consider capturing the Nasiris as the settlement of their dues to us."

"But we have to try," I said to Jeriad.

"There must be something that we could offer in return... an exchange?" my mother suggested.

Both Aisha and Jeriad looked doubtful.

"I'm not sure what on earth would entice Cyrus enough to give up my family," Aisha said miserably. "Certainly no amount of material wealth."

"I have a suggestion." Jeriad spoke up, standing and beginning to pace up and down. "While it would not be wise to ask them to relinquish the Nasiris, perhaps... just perhaps... the Drizans themselves would agree to help you fulfill the fae's demands."

That was certainly an interesting proposition. We had to hope that the dragons really did have enough sway left for the Drizans to agree to such a favor.

"Then what about my family?" Aisha asked, looking

distraught.

"I do not know, maiden," Jeriad replied, his brows furrowed.

I turned to Aisha, actually feeling compassion toward her. Too much had happened since my stay in The Oasis for me to continue seeing her as the annoying, jealous teenage girl she'd always conducted herself as.

"Aisha," I said, placing a hand on her shoulder, hoping to offer at least a little comfort. "We need to just take this one step at a time."

BEN

It was decided that we would return to The Dunes via the portal in Lake Nasser. Aisha assured us that this was the best way to reach the realm of jinn. I recalled traveling through that portal with Aisha and being curious about the strange world of black sand we'd landed in on the other side. At the time she'd brushed it off and not revealed the truth about where we were.

So that was where we needed to head. Back to Egypt. Back to where all of this had started.

Armed with this single idea of Jeriad's—clearly the brightest idea any of us had—we decided who would come and who would stay behind. I was deeply touched—though not by any means surprised—by how many were willing to embark on this mission. The lineup expanded to sixteen, and ended up consisting of: myself and River, whom I didn't even bother trying to dissuade from coming; Aisha; my parents; Jeriad and three other dragons, Ridan, Neros and Tyron; Marcilla, Chantel and Nolan— being fae they could be useful; my sister and Caleb; and finally Lucas and Jeramiah, whom we could hardly expect to want to be separated so soon after their reunion. No witches could come with us, of course, despite how useful they might be. As for Aisha, although she couldn't enter The Dunes, she could wait outside the realm's boundaries and be a source of information.

I was sure that Aiden and Kailyn would have wanted to come, but wherever they were on the island now, we weren't about to fetch them. Besides, my grandfather had been through enough recently. He deserved a break.

We made hurried preparations to leave and headed to the Port, where the dragons shifted into their beastly forms.

I picked up River and settled us both on Jeriad's back, behind his neck, while Rose and Caleb settled behind us, further toward the dragon's tail. The others—including Aisha—spread themselves among the remaining dragons.

I placed River in front of me, with her back against my chest and my legs on either side of her, keeping her secure.

I wrapped one arm around her waist while my other hand gripped the scales of the dragon. I could've flown alongside the dragons, of course, but I wanted to take every opportunity to stay close to River.

The sun had already dipped by now so it did not give discomfort to the vampires among us. The dragons lifted into the sky and picked up speed until we'd flown past the island's boundary.

Shooting up through a layer of clouds, we emerged beneath a ceiling of twinkling stars. River and I found ourselves with another quiet moment. My right hand traveled up from her waist to the base of her neck. I tilted her head back gently, leaning it over my shoulder, and tasted her lips. She ran her fingers through my hair, pulling me closer.

I realized that she must be cold. She wasn't wearing warm clothes, and we were flying with great speed and altitude, which made it hard to benefit much from the dragons' body heat. My body, although not exactly hot, was not cold either. It was lukewarm, which I guessed was better than nothing. I twisted her around so that she faced me, and she wrapped her legs around my waist. I engulfed her in my arms, rubbing her back with my palms in an attempt to warm her, while trailing my lips from the top of her forehead down along the bridge of her nose. She huddled closer to me, gathering her arms against my chest, and rested her cheek against my collarbone.

River. My fiancée. It still hadn't quite hit home.

"I love you," I whispered. It felt like I couldn't say it enough. Knowing what could happen in just a matter of days...

She kissed the base of my throat before resting her head against me again. "I could live forever like this," she breathed back. "Perched on this dragon. With you. Here. Now."

"Me too," I replied.

Her eyelids kissed closed, and a smile spread across her face. I rested my chin above her head, still stroking her back to warm her. At some point during the ride, she managed to fall asleep. That she felt safe enough in my arms to accomplish such a feat atop a dragon, with no safety belts and hundreds of feet of freefall on either side of us, made my heart soar.

Rose and Caleb moved closer to us, and I began to talk to them in a low tone, answering all the many questions they both had. I remained holding River all the while, my hands slowly roaming the contours of her back and waist. And I felt fuller than I ever had in my life.

When the dragons began descending, River woke by herself.

"Looks like we've arrived," Rose said.

River lifted her head from my shoulder and gazed around, bewildered. It took her a few moments to remember where we were.

The dragons descended rapidly and soon a sprawling lake came into view. Lake Nasser. As the dragons touched down on a small islet, I gathered River to me and the four of us slid off the shifter's back. I held back with River as everyone piled through the portal. Then, holding hands, River and I leapt in together. As we darted through the abyss, I molded my limbs around her so that by the time we flew out, I was able to give her a soft landing. Not that it would have been hard, anyway. The Dunes appeared to consist of nothing but a massive, coal-black desert.

Aisha, having been unable to exit on this side, was still stuck within the portal. And there she would have to remain. She gazed at us sadly.

"Come back and tell me what's going on as soon as you've spoken to the Drizans," she said anxiously.

I nodded, though I could not promise that we'd be able to fulfill that request.

Aisha pointed us toward the right direction, while Jeriad walked up front, leading us across the desert. The dragons ended up taking flight again to spot the entrance to the Drizans' lair. Once they'd found it, they returned to us, allowing us to resume our positions on their backs, and transported us the rest of the distance. We touched down on the sand again outside a giant golden medallion in the shape of a scorpion etched into the ground. Their entrance.

My father, being closest to the door, drummed his fists against it before stepping back. Tense silence followed. I cast my eyes behind me, expecting to see Lucas cowering at the back. But he wasn't. I spotted him with his son a few feet away from my father, obscured by Jeriad's towering form.

A loud creak snapped my attention back to the golden entrance. It swung open. Out floated a tall male jinni with wild black curls for hair and diamond necklaces adorning his dark, muscled chest. His hazel eyes roamed us, and his jaw positively dropped open as he spied me, Lucas, and the other three fae.

Jeriad was the first to speak. "We are here to see King Cyrus."

The jinni's eyes remained on the fae in our group, even as he shook his head and replied to the dragon, "Not with these creatures." He prodded a finger toward us.

"These are my friends and are of no danger to you, but of course, that's not a problem," Jeriad replied, twisting his head to shoot me a glare.

Taking my cue, I immediately backed away—pulling

River with me—and the other fae followed me.

I wasn't sure what the Drizans had against fae, but this sure was not a good start.

DEREK

Based on the look the jinni had given Ben, Lucas and the other fae, I was already expecting the worst, and from the grim look on Jeriad's face, so was he. The Drizan guard led us down through their ornate palace until we reached Cyrus' throne room, which we had visited once before. It was empty now, and we all bundled inside, waiting for the king.

The imposing jinni burst through the door a few minutes later, wearing a golden crown laced with hibiscus, and floated toward us. He had grown a thick beard since we'd last seen him, and he flashed us a broad smile, revealing thick, gold-plated teeth. Apparently he was in a good mood. *Something that can only help...*

He stopped before Jeriad. "What brings you back so soon?" he asked, his voice rich and hearty.

"I have come to request a real favor from you this time, Cyrus," Jeriad said.

Cyrus cocked his head. "A real favor? And what might you mean by that?"

"Collecting the Nasiris, as I'm sure you'll agree, was not entirely a favor since there was such great interest in it for you." Jeriad's tone remained polite, yet assertive.

"I suppose that is true enough," Cyrus conceded. "I might be willing to do you a favor, depending on what it is."

He drifted up to his giant throne and took his seat, his beady eyes roaming us like an eagle's.

Jeriad looked at me and nodded slightly, indicating that I begin my explanation. Taking a step forward, I began to recount our predicament as told by my son, even as countless questions rose in my own mind. *What do the fae want with the jinn anyway? And for that matter, what exactly are fae?* Ben had returned as one, but otherwise I had never heard of such creatures except in fairytales.

As soon as I mentioned the fae, Cyrus held up a hand and lifted from his chair.

"We cannot help you."

I stared at him, my heart sinking. "What do you mean?"

"We do not work with fae, in any way, shape or form."

He turned back to Jeriad. "I'm sorry, noble dragon. But you'll have to search elsewhere."

"Then would you free the Nasiris instead?" Sofia blurted next to me.

I winced, already anticipating Cyrus' response even before he turned on Sofia and looked her over coldly. "The Nasiris are ours, fair lady," he said. His voice had turned to ice. He never had liked Sofia. Not since she had tried to interfere with his assault on Nuriya back in The Oasis.

"You wouldn't agree to spare... anyone at all?" she pressed. "Not even two or three?"

To this, Cyrus did not bother to even respond. He simply roamed toward the exit, calling over his shoulder another apology to Jeriad for being unable to help.

As he left through the door, the same guard who had escorted us down here returned to the room before stating the obvious. "I believe the meeting is over."

BEN

After the fae, River and I had retreated, we waited about a mile away for the rest to emerge. In this flat landscape, we caught sight of them as soon as they climbed out from the trapdoor. We hurried over to them and bombarded them with questions.

As expected, all had not gone well in the meeting with Cyrus. Clearly, the Drizans had some kind of long-standing feud with the fae that Aisha didn't know about. They seemed to despise them as much as they despised witches.

That meant we were back to square one. Our original plan. Although it could hardly be called a plan when none of us had a clue how to pull it off.

We traveled with the dragons back to the portal,

remembering our promise to keep Aisha informed. Her mournful face lit up a little on spotting us approaching the abyss, and then a little more after we told her what had happened.

"So we need to rescue my family after all," she murmured.

Since I had already suspected that the Drizans would not come through, I'd already been thinking ahead to our next step while the others met with Cyrus. I figured that, before anything else, I should assume my subtle form and try to get a better scope of the palace and locate the Nasiris. But first, I wanted to know as much as possible about the Drizans' lair. The first question that sprang to my mind to ask Aisha was whether they had some kind of protective barrier over the palace, like The Oasis had, and like we had in The Shade. Aisha assured me that they didn't, as it was a way of showing their dominance over all jinn tribes.

"Where do you think your family could be?" I asked next.

Aisha swallowed hard. "I hate to think… They could be kept in the prison on the lower floors, or they could be kept as servants on the higher floors."

"Okay," I said, clenching my jaw. "I'll just have to look around. If I was invisible, would they have some other way of detecting me?"

Aisha looked uncertain, but replied, "I don't think so. Not if you don't make any noise, or do anything else to draw attention to yourself."

River's hold around my hand tightened. "Are you sure you're going by yourself?" she asked me quietly. "Why don't you take one of the other fae with you?"

"While we have no clear plan, it's best only one person goes down there to scope the place out." I kissed her cool cheek before turning to the rest of them, nodding grimly. "I'll be careful."

"Don't you dare get caught, Ben," Rose said sternly.

"Yeah…"

I drifted away from the group, flying over the sand, back in the direction of the Drizans' palace. As much as I hated to, I willed my body to thin until I was invisible, feeling like a ghost again. I'd no idea how I'd even made the transformation, just as, now that I thought about it, I had no idea how I'd actually moved my old body. As a human or vampire, when I'd wanted to stretch out an arm, I would just stretch out an arm. Making myself invisible as a fae was no more difficult.

I soon approached the medallion entrance. Steeling myself, I sank down into the door and emerged on the other side in an eye-wateringly lavish entrance chamber studded with gems and diamonds whose total value—for all I knew— could have been hundreds of millions of dollars. As I continued my way into the Drizans' palace, the senseless luxury only increased. I found myself wondering just how many other tribes they'd ransacked along the way to amass such riches.

I traveled slowly at first, careful to stop every time I saw a passing jinni and keep close to the wall until they passed. Then, after several minutes of navigating the corridors, which thankfully weren't all that busy, I gained a little more confidence.

The Nasiris. Where are they?

I searched the entirety of the top floor, consisting mostly of communal areas, grand dining halls and sitting rooms, before descending to a more residential area on the level beneath. As I passed through gorgeous apartments, it was clear why the corridors hadn't been crowded. It was night-time, and jinn apparently turned in just as humans did.

Finally, as I neared the second to last apartment on my level, I caught sight of a familiar face floating in my direction. Safi, if I remembered correctly. Aisha's sister, and the cook whose bony meal River had upchucked.

She was trailing down the hallway toward me. Her youthful face looked tired and worn. She wore nothing but a red silken one-piece to cover her chest, while silver manacles hugged her wrists. Clasped in her hands was a golden tray holding a goblet filled with a deep purple liquid. And tattooed into her bare right arm was the emblem of a black scorpion. *How the tables have turned.*

My first instinct was to speak to her, but I wasn't confident enough that we wouldn't be heard. I didn't know who might be lurking around the corner. So I simply followed as she made her way down the corridor, then took a sharp left before turning into a doorway. She closed the door behind her and I slid through, even as I shuddered at the sensation. It reminded me horribly of being a ghost.

Emerging on the other side ahead of me, Safi traveled deeper into the apartment. She stopped outside a door and knocked.

"Enter," a rumbling male voice called, and I could've sworn that her hands trembled.

She pushed the door open regardless and I followed close behind her before she could shut it on me.

She definitely shuddered now as she approached a king-sized bed, upon which lay a jinni who possessed all the overbearing features of a Drizan. He was bare-chested, his head leaning casually against the headboard. He looked over Safi with mild amusement before he reached out a hand to accept the goblet she'd bent down to offer him. He drank deep, and then, discarding the glass, pulled Safi into his bed and slid her next to him beneath the sheets.

I felt sick to my stomach. The worst part was feeling that I couldn't do anything to help her. Blowing my cover now would be the most foolish thing I could do. It could be suicide for the two of us. I still didn't know what these jinn were capable of, and other than the ability to switch between subtle and physical states, I didn't even know what—if any other—powers I had.

I turned to leave. I had to keep searching for another Nasiri—one I would hopefully find on their own so I could talk to them.

If Safi was up in these higher levels, perhaps some of the others were too, and they hadn't all been thrown in prison.

I roamed from chamber to chamber, coming across many more Drizans, before noticing my surroundings becoming even more lavish, barely an inch of the wall not covered with some kind of elaborate display of rubies and diamonds. Perhaps I was nearing the quarters of the royal family themselves.

My suspicion was confirmed on entering the largest, most breathtaking apartment I'd entered so far. I heard female voices drifting from one of the rooms.

"How could you, Cyrus?" They were giggling.

Following the voices, I entered a stately bedroom, where sprawled in the center of the bed was a man who lived up to every description I'd heard of Cyrus. He was a dark beast of a man. King of the Drizans... he certainly lived like one.

He'd turned his quarters into a harem, with dozens of beautiful female jinn fawning over him.

Seeing all these women around him while he drew one in for a deep kiss every now and then, I still wasn't sure how certain… bodily functions even worked with jinn, given that they had no lower half. I wasn't left pondering the conundrum long, however, as I realized that one of the women surrounding Cyrus was none other than Nuriya. She'd been obscured from view by another jinni—who'd been leaning over to drop pomegranate seeds into Cyrus' mouth—but now I saw her, perched near the edge of the bed. Her wrists were manacled like Safi's, only instead of silver, Nuriya's cuffs were gold. The poor woman was dressed just as scantily as Safi was and, as striking as her face was, her eyes appeared dull, drained of life. She bore the same black scorpion tattoo on her arm.

Cyrus reached out a hand and planted it beside her on the mattress. Unfortunately for her, I wasn't the only one who'd noticed her indifference.

"What's wrong now, Nuri?" Cyrus drawled, and I realized now that his eyes rolled slightly. He was intoxicated.

Ugh, as my sister would say.

"Massage me," he insisted, spreading out his palm. She eyed his hand with resignation before taking it between her fingers and kneading it.

I felt oddly protective of Nuriya—who, in spite of everything, had helped me during one of the darkest times of my life. My hands were itching to wallop the man with one of the burning torches that hung from his walls.

But, even as I clenched my fists, all I could do was leave. Again.

I still haven't found a Nasiri on their own… Maybe I really did need to go deeper for that.

After what felt like another quarter hour of roaming, I spied another female jinni who looked familiar to me, and who bore the scorpion tattoo. I'd seen her face somewhere around The Oasis, but had never spoken to her. Like Safi, her manacles were silver, and also like Safi, she appeared to be bringing something to her new master. She held a small pot of heavily scented ointment. Massage oil, no doubt. Since the corridor was empty and I was painfully aware of every minute I wasted in this place, this time I dared take a chance. I willed myself to solidify a little so that she could see me and planted myself in front of her. Her mouth hung open as she stared at me and I feared for a moment that she would drop the ointment.

She glanced up and down the corridor before hissing, "What are you doing here?"

At least she recognizes me.

"Trying to free you," I whispered back. "You and your

family."

"It's impossible," she gasped, tears welling in her eyes. "We cannot leave this place."

"What's binding you?" I asked, staring at the chains. They held only her wrists, while the rest of her had free movement. But I'd already had first-hand experience of the power of jinn to imprison their slaves. It was no surprise as she glanced at her tattoo.

"We are bound by a curse… at least, those of us left." A sob escaped her throat.

"What do you mean?"

She brushed her leaking eyes with the back of one hand. "Cyrus, he… he k-killed Bahir. In front of us. In front of Nuriya."

Learning of Bahir's demise came as a blow. I owed my life to that jinni. *Poor man.* I'd never even gotten a chance to thank him.

"I-I have to go," the jinni breathed, glancing around anxiously and beginning to move away.

"Wait," I whispered. "Are you really telling me there's no way for you to escape? There must be some way."

She cast one last fleeting glance at me, her eyes wide with fear. "There's only one way to free us and that is… to slay Cyrus."

After dropping that pile of bricks, she hurried away,

leaving me staring after her.

Slay Cyrus.

Great.

BEN

Returning to the others waiting by the portal, I explained to them what I'd learned from one of the female jinn, albeit leaving out the details about how the Nasiris' family were being treated, for Aisha's sake.

"So," I concluded, "we need to kill Cyrus."

My words were met with silence. Jeriad, disappointingly, didn't have any advice to offer. Even Aisha had pursed her lips.

"Well?" I asked the shifter and the jinni. "Don't you have any ideas?"

"He would kill you first," Aisha said.

"But jinn *can* be killed?" I pressed.

"Of course they can be killed," Aisha said, rolling her eyes as though it was the most obvious thing in the world. "They can be killed, just like any supernatural can be ended, but only while they are manifested in their physical forms. Flesh and bone. You could stab one in the chest, chop off the head; there are boundless options, but... Cyrus? Not only does he possess powers above all other jinn, his physical prowess is second to none."

I paused, mulling over her words. "What if I just snuck up on him while he was asleep and slit his throat? That would kill him?"

"Yes," Aisha said. "But I assure you, it would not be that simple."

"It's the same with ghouls," Marcilla murmured behind me. "They can only be killed when they're in their solid state."

"So we need to pick a moment when Cyrus is in his solid state," I said, thinking back to when I had seen him just now. At least his top half had been manifest—and seemed solid. The thought gave way to another question that had been at the back of my mind ever since I'd first laid eyes on jinn.

"Why are your bottom halves perpetually covered by mist?" I asked Aisha. "Or do you not have bottom halves?"

She sighed, glancing down at her own wispy lower body. "We do. But we keep them covered because, well, it's just

44

the way of the jinn. Tradition, if you like. We keep our lower half hidden from everyone but our sworn life partner. In most cases that means a husband or wife."

I never would've guessed that was the reason. If chastity was their concern, I wondered why they could not just cover up with clothes, like humans did. But who was I to judge? "I see," I said, my eyes roaming her smoky trail. "So you do have legs and feet, just like humans?"

"Uh-huh," Aisha said.

"Okay." My curiosity satisfied, I shook away the thought and turned my mind back to more important matters. "So I will need to follow Cyrus around and wait for him to turn his back, or something... I guess..." I was grasping at straws.

"Remember that you will also have to assume a solid form in order to kill his," Aisha said. "And I suspect that, like jinn and ghoul, fae can also be killed in their physical bodies."

That was something I had not even considered yet. Of course, I would need to be solid in order to assault him in the first place.

"Remember his superlative powers," Aisha went on. "While you... well, to be honest, I don't even know if fae have any powers. I don't know much about them."

That makes two of us. I turned to Marcilla and raised a brow, hoping she might have something to add.

The werewolf-turned-fae shrugged. "I don't know

everything," she replied.

I wished now that I had stopped to ask Sherus for more details about this body, but at the time, I'd simply been too elated to think straight. We all had.

I sat down at the edge of the crater, in front of River. She wrapped her arms around me, pulling her chest against my back, and I felt her lips press against me gently. Everyone else remained quiet. What could they say? All of us were in the dark. I covered my face with my hands and tried to think. The way my mind whirled with conflicting thoughts and ideas, it felt as though River was the only thing grounding me.

But a few minutes later, I had found my answer. As much as I loathed even considering it, there was only one clear next step on this path. Before attempting anything, we needed to learn more about Cyrus and his weaknesses. It would be foolish to try to murder him without doing so. There was a reason why he was so feared in the land of jinn. Neither I nor any of us could dive in blind.

This meant I had to pay yet another visit to the oracle. The same person who had caused me to almost lose my soul to The Underworld... yet to whom I also owed my escape, and this body I found myself in now.

But can I really stand facing that woman again?

I didn't have the luxury of choice.

BEN

There was no point in our whole group going to visit Hortencia. So although we all traveled back through the portal to Lake Nasser, it was decided that only Aisha, River and me would go.

I couldn't have been more grateful that we had Aisha with us. Not only did she know how to locate Hortencia's cave, she also found the strength to vanish the three of us there, which saved God knew how much of our precious time.

We appeared outside the entrance to the cave—a cave that was rather familiar to me by now. I moved forward first, holding River's hand and pulling her down the narrow passageway leading to the oracle's front door, while Aisha followed behind us. I knocked three times.

When there had been no reply after ten seconds, I called her name, "Hortencia!"

Still no reply.

"Hortencia!" I called again, more loudly, my voice resounding off the tunnel walls.

I pressed my ear against the door. I couldn't hear a sound. Not even breathing.

As much as I'd been dreading the idea of coming face to face with the oracle again and trying to make sense of her winding words, I couldn't help but feel a surge of panic now. *Is she all right? What's happened?*

"Let me go in," Aisha said. She vanished.

River's and my breathing was uneven as we waited in tense silence. A few seconds passed before the door opened; it was Aisha, letting us into an otherwise vacant room.

River and I stepped inside and gazed around. For a moment I feared that perhaps somebody had managed to kidnap the oracle and done something with her—after all, she was a most valuable asset to any race of supernatural—but there appeared to be no signs of struggle here. On the contrary, the few possessions the oracle had—a few pots, an old stove, her orbs and other strange artifacts—were neatly tucked away. It looked tidier than I'd ever seen it. The orderliness gave a chilling sense of finality to the emptiness of the room.

My throat dry, I looked from River to Aisha. "Where could she have gone?" I breathed.

Aisha looked just as bewildered as me. "I've no idea. She… She's always been here. At least, every time I've visited. I wonder if maybe she went to visit her sister, Pythia."

"Where does Pythia live?" I asked, my stomach twisting in knots. It made me sick to think of the time passing. We had just over a day left.

"I don't know where she lives," Aisha said, shrugging.

Cursing beneath my breath, I was about to grab River's hand and leave the empty quarters when she pointed to a little package set atop a ledge. We'd been so distracted by the oracle's absence, it hadn't been noticed until now.

I walked over to it and picked it up. The wrapping was made of parchment, and within it was something weighty. I unfurled the paper and a tiny glass vial containing vivid green liquid dropped into my palm. Then I caught sight of four words scrawled across the parchment in burgundy ink:

Drink deep, curious fairy.

BEN

Curious fairy. Grimacing, I handed the vial to Aisha. The oracle always did have a way with words.

"What do you think this is?" I asked the jinni.

Aisha examined the vial with a deep frown on her face. "She knew that you were coming for more answers," she murmured. She opened the lid, sniffed the potion, and wrinkled her nose.

"Well?" I asked. I'd had enough dealings with vials of liquid to make me averse to drinking anything out of a bottle for the rest of my life.

"I'm not sure," Aisha replied, replacing the cap.

"Well, you can't just drink it, Ben," River said, taking the bottle from Aisha and examining it herself.

And yet the oracle knew I was coming for answers... and she told me to drink it.

I'd already resigned myself to the fact that the fastest way forward would be to consult the oracle—despite how maddening she could be. And here was her note, giving me a direct instruction... I'd just been to hell and back. Could anything really be worse than that?

"I guess beggars can't be choosers," I muttered, taking the potion from River's hands.

As I took a seat in a rickety chair, River's face drained of all color. I hated to do this to her, but I had no choice. If we stood a chance of having a future together, we had to take risks.

I removed the cap and, raising the bottle to my lips, downed it in one shot.

An unbearable bitterness overwhelmed my taste buds and stung my tongue, but before I could even gag, my vision started to fade. I felt myself falling backward and I guessed that I would have toppled off the chair, but I couldn't know for sure. My consciousness was elsewhere.

Darkness enshrouded me, but then there was light. A dim, flickering light. Like candlelight. As if a lens had just focused, I found myself in another cave, quite distinct from the one I'd just left. It was larger, with a concave ceiling. And it was bare except for a burning torch that hung from one wall, a glass flask of murky water, a bundle of tattered blankets on the sharp, rocky ground, and an old, eyeless woman, wearing a long dark dress—the signature garb of the oracle. But this... this was not the oracle I had met. Hortencia, although horribly disfigured, had still appeared youthful. Her face was unlined, as though she was no older than twenty-five. I imagined that if Hortencia had eyes, her face might've even been pretty, in a pixie-like way.

This woman's face was as shriveled as a hundred-year-old's, her form bent and crooked.

"Who are you?" I whispered.

The woman slid slowly off the rock and padded with bare feet across the sharp ground toward me. Her skin looked thin. I was sure the rocks would cut her soles. "You know me," she rasped, her lips curving in a knowing smile.

"Hortencia?" I asked. *Who else could it be?*

"It is me," she said. "Always me."

"What... What happened to you?"

"I left," she said simply. "And I will not be returning. But I did not abandon you. I saw that your needy self would come for me, and so we meet like this."

I was surprised that she had taken the trouble to leave that note and vial for me. In her eyes at least, Hortencia owed me nothing. On the contrary, I owed her. In fact, I wasn't really sure why she bothered to help any supernaturals at all. Maybe it was just for her own amusement.

As I gazed around the chamber, I wanted to ask what "this" even was—where were we? But before I could, the oracle continued, "So you trusted me enough to drink the juice."

Trust might be too flattering a word. "I had no choice," I said through gritted teeth.

She grinned, folds of her sagging skin bunching beneath her cheekbones. "Good," she croaked. "You are learning. You are learning."

Learning what? I would have asked, but I had more burning questions. "I need to know about Cyrus," I said. *Though, of course, you already know that.*

Hortencia let out a deep cackle, which spiraled into a violent coughing fit. She dropped to her knees, her hands grasping the rocks as she hacked and spat. I was holding my breath as she looked up again.

What on earth happened to her?

She summoned the flask of stale water and drank from it. Then she folded her legs in front of her and sat cross-legged where she'd fallen. She patted the ground next to her. "Sit," she commanded me. As I lowered myself, she smiled again— a sickly sweet smile—and said, "It's story time."

I nodded, waiting tensely for her to start.

"Close your eyes and concentrate on my words," she said. She reached out a hand and trailed her clammy fingers from the top of my forehead down to my eyelids, forcing them closed. Then, removing her hand, she began...

"Once upon a time in the land of jinn, there lived a mighty king known as Harzad Drizan. Like his father and grandfather, Harzad was a ruthless leader. He built upon the work of his ancestors to forge a path toward establishing the Drizans as the most prominent tribe in The Dunes. He ruled with an iron fist, and his people respected him, while all other tribes cowered in his wake... except for the Gheens. Although a smaller tribe than the Drizans, the Gheens were highly intelligent and fiercely tenacious, bowing to no-one.

"As the years passed, and Harzad's two sons grew into men, having children of their own, the time came for Harzad to relinquish his reign—as is the custom of jinn. The Gheens were still unvanquished, and Harzad knew how great a challenge his reigning son would have to face as king.

"His older son was Trezus, while his younger was Cyrus. As was the tradition with royal siblings, the role of leader did not automatically go to the eldest. It went to whomever rose victorious in a treacherous contest, arranged by the king himself to determine true worthiness of the throne.

"Harzad's father, Setir, had done the same to him and his three brothers, and Harzad's grandfather had done the same to Setir. And as was also the custom among Drizans, the stakes of each generation's test had to be raised. The tasks would get harder, more impossible, for this was the way that they ensured their rulers only went from strength to strength, and never weakened.

"Harzad took his time in selecting the task and eventually, with the help of his counsel, he came up with what he believed to be the perfect idea.

"The Drizans were famed for their affinity for The Dunes' native scorpions. Creatures the size of small horses, with looming, venomous stingers and pincers strong enough to squish a man's skull like butter. Harzad's great-grandfather had taken in a large horde of these scorpions and bred them in captivity. Using his unparalleled powers, he had experimented with numerous mutations until he came upon the perfect variation to employ as additional security for their lair. By the end, he'd managed to make their venom so potent, a single sting could kill a jinni in a matter of seconds if caught in their physical form... unless the jinni was exceptionally strong. Only one had been known to survive the sting, and that was the leader of the Gheens.

"In those days the Drizans' prominence was less established, and the creatures were of use for a number of years. Once the Drizans had secured their supremacy among the jinn, Harzad's ancestor released a number back into the wild, where they continued to breed uninhibited.

"It was these wild scorpions that Harzad used for his task. Trezus and Cyrus were to battle in an arena with two male scorpions—one each—slaying the monsters, and then drinking the venom from their stingers in front of the gathered crowds. There would be only two rules: the upper halves of their bodies must remain in a physical state, and they weren't allowed to use magic. Whoever survived both the battle and the venom would be crowned that very same day. If it became a draw, then Harzad would be forced to think up another worthy challenge.

"The brothers were each given four days to prepare for the task—however they chose to do so, using either brain or brawn—and went their separate ways.

"Trezus immediately summoned the clan's physician and spent the first two days developing an antidote that could line his stomach against the poison. Then the next two days he spent in the armory, gathering and training with the most lethal weapons.

"His younger brother Cyrus, on the other hand, disappeared. He vanished the same hour the men were given the task and he remained absent the entire four days. Nobody knew where he went, not a single one of his wives or children. But on the night of the contest, when the two men were due to meet for the contest, Trezus arrived bearing antidotes and weapons, while Cyrus came with nothing at all. Not even a shield to cover his exposed chest.

"His father was both surprised and saddened; Cyrus had always been his favorite of the two. Trezus was only encouraged, thinking that his brother's arrogance would surely lead to his demise.

"The king, queen and all the Drizan people gathered in a makeshift arena in the desert, with the two brothers standing on either side. Two jinn let loose the first mammoth black scorpion a few feet in front of Trezus—who had volunteered to go first.

"As the scorpion hurtled toward Trezus, he valiantly swung and swiped with his swords, but he was unable to get close enough to gouge the scorpion, so ferociously protected by pincers and a towering stinger. In the end, he managed to spear through a joint in its neck—paralyzing it—but when Trezus severed the stinger from the dying scorpion and squeezed the venom into his mouth, he collapsed instantaneously. The attendant physicians gathered round, but they were too late. Trezus Drizan had not been strong enough to withstand the poison. He was not worthy of his father's crown.

"All eyes turned on Cyrus. Two jinn brought in the second scorpion and placed it in front of Cyrus. It scuttled toward him, just as the other had done to Trezus, but as it reached within four feet of the younger brother, it stopped abruptly. The ringmasters gathered round, suspicious that Cyrus could be playing foul and using supernatural powers, but they soon verified he was not.

"The scorpion remained still, pincers folded, stinger hanging low, as was its head. It was as though the beast was bowing to the young man. And then, with one swift movement, Cyrus launched onto the back of the scorpion, took its stinger within his muscular arms and snapped it from its body. He leapt off as the scorpion flailed and rolled onto its back. Shortly after, the supervisors pronounced it dead.

"The crowd held their breath as Cyrus bit right into the barbed stinger, tearing through the flesh until he reached the venom, where he poured a full mouthful into his jaws for all to see. He swallowed... and yet he stood.

"A minute passed. Two minutes. Three minutes.

"Still he stood.

"The crowd erupted, the king and queen relieved, and all present hailed their new king as a miracle. A gift from God Himself. Harzad simply labeled him as the son he'd always known he had, a true heir to his throne.

"Cyrus' coronation ceremony was the most lavish in the history of the Drizans. And so began Cyrus' rule. Even more ruthless than his father, after only four years, he eradicated the Gheens as any potential threat. But throughout Cyrus' years of ruling, until this very day, he never revealed to anybody how he truly came to power. How he truly withstood the test his older brother could not. And why should people question him, when by his actions he was so clearly meant to lead?"

The oracle's voice faded. I opened my eyes—or at least my mind's eye. Her head was tilted toward me thoughtfully, the torchlight sending shadows dancing across her wizened face.

"Well?" I said. "What did happen to Cyrus during those four days? What did he do? What has given him the strength that he has?"

I should've expected what was coming the minute she stopped talking at such a pivotal moment in the story.

"Benjamin, Benjamin," she said, with an almost gleeful smile. "You like to be spoon fed, don't you?"

I like straight answers, the same as any person who is not insane.

But I already sensed that I was going to get nothing of the sort from the oracle. Her outward appearance might've changed drastically, but she was still the same maddening woman.

"I will give you what you need, not what you think you need," she said after a pause. "And what you need is my advice."

Advice. The last time she'd given me her "advice", I'd ended up trafficked to The Underworld and imprisoned as an ornamental pet.

"What is your *advice*?" I asked, my jaw tight.

She rose to her feet. Her withered, almost unrecognizable face panned down to me as she replied, "Return to The Drizans' palace and remember… everybody has something to hide."

BEN

Before I could pose another question, the scene around me faded, as did the oracle. I found myself lying on the ground. I opened my eyes. My real eyes. River was crouching over me, one palm against my forehead. Aisha hovered nearby, too.

"Are you okay?" River asked anxiously. "You were talking to yourself."

I sat up, rubbing my head, livid at the oracle for having sent me back without any explanation as to what she'd meant. It took a few moments to collect my thoughts before standing up again.

"We need to return to Lake Nasser." I sighed. "I'll tell you everything when we get there."

Aisha was strong enough to transport us back to the islet where we'd left the others, and on arrival I recounted what had happened to River, Aisha and myself.

"So you've got to return to the Drizans' palace," my father murmured.

"Yes. I have to observe some more..." *And hope against hope the oracle isn't messing with me.*

"You'll really go alone again?" River asked.

Before I could answer, Lucas stepped forward. "I'll go with you," he said, eyeing me steadily.

My parents spun around and gazed at him in shock. I couldn't miss the flash of gratefulness in their eyes, while I could not say the same for Jeramiah. The last thing he wanted was to let his father go again, naturally.

"Okay," I told Lucas. I wasn't exactly sure why he had volunteered but I was grateful. I didn't think it was a good idea to go down with any more than two, but two of us should be manageable.

Lucas and I left the islet, even as the expression on River's face cut me to the core. We dove through the portal and arrived back in The Dunes.

We zoomed to the entrance of the Drizans' lair and, in our subtle forms, passed through the scorpion entrance, which, after the oracle's tale, now held new meaning for me. As I led Lucas onward, the palace was much quieter than before. We didn't spot a single jinni in the hallways. I guessed because it was so early in the morning.

We approached Cyrus' apartment and entered it. I headed straight for the bedroom where we'd left him. No laughter drifted from it now, but rather deep heavy snoring. We drifted inside to see Cyrus lying in the middle of his giant bed, beneath silk sheets, with Nuriya—apparently also sleeping—clutched to his chest. The other female jinn had gone.

Lucas and I roamed silently about the large chamber before exploring the rest of the apartment—which was like a palace in itself. It took us a surprisingly long time to explore every corner of it. We spotted nothing of particular interest, just more of the same, senseless luxury.

We returned to the bedroom again, the couple was still sound asleep. My eyes traveled over the walls, settling on a display of bejeweled daggers. *What if I just tried to kill him now? In his sleep? Wouldn't it be easy?*

Lucas and I—transparent, though still visible to each other—exchanged glances. I sensed that he had guessed what was going through my mind. His expression was uncertain.

Despite everything that I'd been told about Cyrus' powers, and how it would not be easy to end him, I couldn't stop myself from at least attempting it… with him lying here so vulnerable. Turning solid, I moved to the daggers and silently removed one from its holder.

Stilling my breathing, I moved closer to the bed, tightening my hold around the blade's handle.

He was so close. *All it might take is a slash across the neck, and this whole nightmare could be over…*

But as soon as I reached the edge of the bed frame, the jinni stirred. Then, to my horror, he twisted away from Nuriya. I barely had time to even think how to react. I thinned myself in an instant and dropped to the floor, causing the dagger to clatter down with me. Lucas had dropped too, and together we raced for the door.

Detaching himself from Nuriya, Cyrus crawled over the bed, peering over the edge at the fallen dagger. He let out a low growl and his dark, dangerous eyes flashed as they darted around the room, his nostrils flaring.

"Who goes there?" he hissed.

We sank through the door, hoping he hadn't spotted us. Emerging on the other side of the door, I whispered my uncle's name.

"We need to leave the apartment," I breathed to my uncle.

I caught sounds of Cyrus tearing through the rooms in search of the intruder as we sank through the walls and arrived back in an outside hallway.

If Cyrus had detected my silent approach through the depths of his sleep, I could only imagine his reflexes when awake.

Lucas and I hurried onward, creating more and more distance between us and that jinni. Eventually we paused in a quiet corner of what appeared to be a dining room.

"What now?" Lucas whispered, his breathing uneven.

The oracle's "advice" rang in my head. *"Remember... everybody has something to hide."*

I clenched my jaw. "We have to keep watching."

BEΠ

We did not dare reenter Cyrus' bedroom, though we had no choice but to return to his apartment. As it turned out, we found him in the kitchen. His back was turned to us, a glass of bright orange liquid in one hand, while the other rested on the marble counter. He drank slowly from the glass, his mind clearly elsewhere… on the strange events of this morning, no doubt.

We watched him finish the glass. Then we followed him as he left the kitchen and returned to the bedroom.

"Nuriya," he said, standing in the doorway.

"Mmh?" an absent voice replied.

"Come," Cyrus said, extending his hand.

Nuriya arrived next to him, and he took her hand, leading her to the kitchen. Opening a silver cabinet, he took down a large flask of the same orange juice he had been drinking. He filled his own glass with it, but this time handed it to Nuriya.

"Drink up, my sweet."

Nuriya still looked bleary-eyed from sleep, or perhaps that was her normal expression now. Obediently she took the glass and sipped. She immediately choked.

"Drink it all," Cyrus insisted.

Gingerly, she swallowed the rest. After setting down the empty glass, she clutched her throat, wincing.

Cyrus looked pleased, his full lips broadening in a smile. Running his palms down her arms, he took her hands in his and leaned forward to kiss her lips.

"You will be my queen, Nuriya. My tenth and final queen."

Tenth and final. Wow… way to woo a woman.

I wondered if all of his nine wives were still current. I also wondered how many children he had fathered. According to the oracle's story, before he was crowned he had already had several wives and children.

Nuriya swallowed harder than when she'd been trying to down the potion. Still, she nodded, though her eyes remained distant.

"I must leave you now," he said. "I have a meeting."

We followed Cyrus out of the kitchen and the apartment, along the winding hallways, until we reached a magnificent courtroom—empty except for one jinni hovering in the centre. He turned around to glare at Cyrus as soon as he entered the room. I could tell immediately from his stark features that he must've been one of Cyrus' relatives, and from his youth, most likely one of his sons.

"Horatio!" Cyrus boomed cheerily.

Horatio. The name rang a bell. I was sure that he was the jinni Aisha had mentioned—her old friend, the person who'd banished her from The Dunes for her own safety. Unless there were two Horatios...

"Father." Horatio stormed over to the king, not even giving his father a chance to rise to his throne. "Are they true, the rumors?" Horatio asked, unrelenting in his glower.

"What rumors?" Cyrus asked, a half amused look on his face.

"That you plan to wed Nuriya?"

Cyrus heaved a sigh. He took to his throne, one elbow resting against its arm, while the other hand massaged his temple.

It seemed that was enough to answer Horatio's question. The young man's eyes narrowed. "You promised my mother she would be your last. You promised us all."

Cyrus' smile faded. "You forget, Horatio, that Nuriya was

meant to bear my heirs long before I made that promise."

"You're an abomination," Horatio spat. "That's what you are."

I was shocked to see Horatio insult Cyrus in this manner, even though he was his son. Horatio must've been very dear to Cyrus, for Cyrus did not admonish him in the slightest. He simply rolled his eyes as his son stormed out of the room.

Crouched down in one corner with Lucas, I dared breathe, "Let's follow him."

Lucas shot me a quizzical look. I jerked my finger toward the door and whizzed toward it.

To have found somebody who did not worship the ground that Cyrus walked on was more than intriguing. Horatio had just become far more interesting than any meeting Cyrus might have been about to call in his court.

We hurried after Horatio as he rushed along winding corridors and then through the doorway of an apartment not far from Cyrus'.

"Mother!" Horatio called, his voice booming through the apartment.

"Horatio?" A female voice drifted from one of the rooms. Horatio turned into a sitting room, where his mother—a beautiful ebony-skinned woman—was seated on a sofa with a servant behind her, brushing her silky black hair with a bejeweled comb.

Her honeycomb eyes widened with concern as her son stormed toward her. His chest heaving, he took a deep breath. "It's true what they're saying. He will wed Nuriya."

Although the news clearly came as a blow to his mother, she did not appear surprised by it.

"What are you going to do?" Horatio asked.

She furrowed her brows. "What do you mean?"

"Are you just going to stand by and say nothing? Father's gone back on his word."

The woman smiled affectionately at her son. Reaching out, she took his hand and held it in hers.

"Darling, we cannot expect that promises will remain unbroken forever." She said the words firmly, as though she was speaking partly to comfort herself about the situation rather than solely for her son's sake. "He carries the destiny of our tribe on his shoulders. Remember that Nuriya was meant to wed Cyrus. Now that he's found her again, his plans to wed her shouldn't come as any surprise. You know the value that she could bring him... that she could bring all of us. The marriage can only strengthen our clan, and that's what we all want, isn't it?"

Fire leapt in Horatio's eyes. "No," he said in a low voice. "That's not what I want."

His mother's eyes widened. "What are you saying?"

"I said that's not what I want!" he shouted. He brought

his fist slamming down against a crystal side table, causing it to shatter.

"Y-you're letting your bias toward the Nasiris blind you, my darling," his mother said. "You never said such things before their arrival. Of course it's only natural you have an attachment to the clan you spent much of your childhood with… but your father has the greater picture in mind."

"A greater picture I want no part of!" Horatio hissed.

With that, he turned on his heel and shot out of the room, leaving his mother shell-shocked.

Lucas and I hurried after the jinni, my interest in him now increased tenfold. He made his way up through the palace until he reached the medallion exit. Pushing it open, he burst out into the desert, his chest still heaving, agitation marring his features.

I wasn't sure where he was planning to go as he went hurtling in the opposite direction, toward the shore. Perhaps merely to blow off some steam. He stopped at the water's edge, arms wrapping around his chest, and gazed out over the sparkling waves.

I looked around to check that nobody had followed him—half expecting his mother to come after him—but no. He was quite alone. *We* were quite alone…

Acutely aware of our escaping time, I didn't stop to consider the consequences of the idea that had just flitted into my brain. I solidified myself behind Horatio and spoke his name.

He whirled around to face me, almost jumping out of his skin.

"What—"

Before he could finish his question, I said, "I'm Aisha's friend."

He was speechless as he gaped at me and then at Lucas, who followed my cue and solidified himself beside me.

"Who are you, and what are you doing here?"

"My name isn't important," I said. "For I am here on the bidding of Aisha Nasiri. She awaits at the other end of the portal, miles north from here. She wishes to speak with you."

His frown grew more severe, although I couldn't miss the flash of anticipation in his eyes. "What about? I-I banished her.... Why would she want to speak with *me*?"

"I'm afraid I do not know," I said, bowing low. "We are only messengers. Will you come with us to see her ladyship?"

Horatio stumbled for words for several moments, narrowing his eyes on us and running a hand through his hair. Finally he shrugged and said, "A-all right. Take me to her."

Clearly his affection for her was—or had been—as strong as I'd hoped for him to agree to come with two strange fae, on the promise of meeting her on the other side of a portal.

But I hadn't expected him to agree quite so easily. And now, as Lucas and I sped with Horatio toward the portal, I found myself wondering what the hell I'd just done.

BEN

My gut was churning as we passed through the gate. My first instinct was to take him to Aisha, because she had a history with him. He had helped her before—albeit against her will—and if anybody had a chance of obtaining information from him, it was her, certainly not me or Lucas. Especially while he was in a mood over his father.

I'd entered the portal first, hoping to have at least a few seconds to warn Aisha of his arrival and what I had just gotten her into. On the other end, I flew out to find everyone sitting among the rocks, looking tense. The dragons had spread their wings to protect the vampires from the sun.

"Horatio," I hissed, barely even having the time to register

River beneath Jeriad's wing, my eyes shooting to Aisha. "He is coming, and—"

I didn't have time to speak another word as he and Lucas darted out of the tunnel.

Horatio straightened and gazed around at our group. As he found Aisha, his deep green eyes softened a touch.

I winced at how shocked Aisha looked. She rose from her resting place beneath a tree, gaping. I hadn't had a chance to even explain to her what I had said. I just had to pray that things worked out for the best.

Horatio moved cautiously toward her. "You... uh, wanted me?" he asked.

Aisha's eyes darted to me. I widened my eyes and mouthed *"Say yes!"*

"Yes," Aisha said, reverting her attention to Horatio. The most unconvincing "yes" that was ever spoken.

Horatio raised a brow, looking around again at our group, before fixing on the dragons. "Why are you with these people?"

Aisha cleared her throat to buy herself some time. "I, uh..." My gut clenched as there was a pause. Then she found her line. "I need my family back," she said, her voice suddenly strained. And I could see from the tears lining her eyes that this was no act.

Horatio ran a hand through his dark curls, rolling his eyes

in exasperation. "I already told you. Your family is in my father's clutches. You need to move on."

"I'd rather die than live without them," she said, her tone bolder this time. "If you won't help me, then at least allow me to try." She planted her hands on her hips, her teary eyes hardening. A frown formed on her pixie-like face. "It's my life. Who are you to decide what I can and cannot do? Remove the ban from me and let me try at least."

"You're insane!" he said, raising his hands in exasperation. "You're young. You still have things to live for. You'll be better off anywhere than back in The Dunes."

"That's for me to decide," she said, teeth gritted. "I want to see my family again."

Horatio pursed his lips, his jaw tightening. Agitation marred his chiseled features, and even a touch of disappointment. "So... So that's all you wanted to see me about. Your family."

"Yes," she replied, her gaze steely. "I want to go to them. The Dunes are just as much my home as yours. Being a Drizan doesn't make you God, you know."

A muscle twitched in Horatio's face and blood rose to his cheeks, as though she'd just slapped him. "I never claimed to be," he murmured. "I was just... trying to protect you."

Aisha's glare didn't relent, and I almost felt in that moment that she was being too harsh on him. He clearly liked her a lot, and I did believe him when he said he'd banished her for her own good.

I also found myself wondering just how he was so much stronger than Aisha that he could banish her from her own realm. Perhaps the Drizans were simply a superior race to the Nasiris in terms of magical prowess.

"All right," Horatio breathed, deflated. Aisha's glare had worn him down. "I'll let you back in but... what exactly do you plan to do? Surely you don't intend to just barge into our palace."

"I need to find a way to free my family," she said. As Horatio began to respond—most likely to repeat his statement that it was not possible—Aisha held up a hand and cut him off. "I don't care what you say. I don't believe there's no way to get them out."

Horatio scoffed. "You've no idea what you're talking about."

"And you're a coward!"

Ouch.

A deathly silence descended upon the islet, Horatio looking as though he'd just been whacked in the gut.

Aisha—unrelenting as an angered bull—charged forward until she was barely two feet away from Horatio. Although she was half his height, her eyes appeared fiery enough to burn holes through Horatio's. "You don't agree with the things that your father's doing. I know it. Yet you've let yourself become... this." With two flicks of her hand, she gestured up and down Horatio's imposing form, looking him over with great disdain. "You're no longer anything like my old friend. You've just become your father's shadow." She paused, her nostrils flaring, then for good measure, added, "Your father's *pawn*." With that she folded her arms over her chest and pursed her lips, her brows knotting in a frown.

Good luck to the man who winds up with this jinni...

Horatio's fists clenched into balls. His breathing became labored, his face so wounded and insulted, his pain was almost tangible.

Aisha's words had hit a raw nerve. Perhaps he realized that he had been a coward. For not standing up to his father, or at least leaving his father's palace. No matter how much he complained to his mother or raged in front of his father, by staying in the palace and being an onlooker, he was essentially a part of his father's atrocities.

The hurt in Horatio's eyes gave way to resentment. His face darkened in a scowl.

"Even if you're right," he breathed, "it doesn't change anything."

"Why not?" Aisha shot back. Her tone hadn't gotten any less severe.

"I cannot go against my father," he said. "My siblings and I only have so much sway. The only thing I could conceivably do is leave, but... he would find me. You do not know me, Aisha—"

"Clearly not," she interjected.

"I have considered these things many times over."

"Then why didn't you attempt any of them?"

"Because it would kill me," he said. "I know my father better than anyone. His leniency, even with his children, only stretches so far and... escaping... my sister Yalisha already tried it."

Recognition sparked in Aisha's eyes. "Yalisha?" she said in a hushed tone. Another childhood friend of hers, I supposed.

Horatio swallowed hard. "He killed her for it."

Whoa.

That silenced the girl.

"We are the children of royalty. Escape would bring humiliation to my father; for how is a king who cannot command obedience from his children ever to be respected by his citizens?"

Aisha found her voice again. "Well... if you don't escape, at least you could help us. I know you don't want my family trapped in there. You don't even have to do anything. Just throw me a bone. Your father would never know."

Horatio swallowed hard. Aisha, suddenly gentle—timid,

even—reached out a hand and touched his arm. Horatio's cheeks flushed.

"Is it true that the only way to my family's freedom… and yours… is to kill your father?" she asked quietly.

Horatio frowned. "Who told you that?"

Aisha cast a furtive look my way before shrugging. "It's a logical assumption," she replied, to my relief. I didn't know how Horatio would react if he knew Lucas and I had been creeping around his home spying.

"Your relatives are bonded to my father, but… I don't think killing him is the *only* way to free them," he said, running his tongue over his lower lip. "But if I ever revealed it to you… his secret… he would not hesitate to murder me with his bare hands."

"I would not want to put you in danger," Aisha said. "But how would he ever know that you told us?"

"Because there are only very few who know. I found out quite by accident. If you acted on the information that I gave you, it wouldn't take him long to suspect me."

Aisha withdrew her hand from his arm, crestfallen.

Horatio, on the other hand, looked conflicted, in spite of his words—as though he were fighting a battle within himself.

He heaved a sigh. "But," he went on, "perhaps I've been a coward long enough." He cleared his throat, gazing down at Aisha. "Maybe... Maybe you're right. Maybe it's time for me to take a stand... regardless of the consequences. If I don't do it now, when will I ever?"

Aisha's eyes brightened. "So you'll tell us? What this mysterious weakness is?"

Thoughtfully, he shook his head. "Rather than telling you, I think it's best that you see it for yourselves..."

BEN

"I think it's best that you see it for yourselves…"

I was burning to ask what "it" meant. But I would have to be patient a little longer.

In the end, not only did Aisha manage to persuade Horatio to lift her ban, he agreed to take us back down to the palace and show us what he was talking about. He said we should get the opportunity to see it today—in less than an hour—for Cyrus was due for his daily visit to one of Horatio's stepmothers. I had no idea what we would witness, but I was just thanking my lucky stars that we finally appeared to be making some progress. Though if our "progress" continued at this slow pace, we were sure to miss our deadline. I had to hope that after this, every progression we made would be far swifter, otherwise all would be in vain. I didn't want to consider the consequences.

I took a moment to kiss River and let my family and the others wish me luck. There was hardly any point in them being here in the first place, but of course I understood why they remained. After having lost me for so long, they wanted to stay as close to me as possible.

I decided that it was best for Lucas to stay behind this time, since Aisha and me accompanying Horatio was enough. The three of us left the islet and returned through the portal. Aisha breathed out in relief as she floated over the black dunes. As hostile as this environment was for her, it was her home after all. We zoomed across the sand and as we neared the palace entrance, Horatio called us to a stop. His eyes roamed Aisha. "You can't come like this, obviously."

"What do you propose?"

"Turn into something. Something small enough for me to carry in my pocket."

"I guess a mouse, again, would make sense," she muttered.

The next thing I knew, Aisha had vanished and on the ground beneath us was a small, brown mouse. Horatio stooped down and picked her up, placing her gently into his pocket. Then grimly, he turned to me.

"It's also time that you thin yourself. As you may know,

jinn cannot see invisible fae just as fae cannot see invisible jinn. I will remain physical, of course, so just make sure not to lose sight of me."

I nodded.

I thinned myself and followed Horatio across the final stretch of sand before the medallion entrance. He opened it and we drifted down the bejeweled staircase into the entrance hall adorned with diamond chandeliers. He began drawing us deeper into the palace, along a route that I'd passed a few times by now. He headed toward his mother's apartment, stopping outside a door a dozen feet before it. Looking up and down the hallway to check that nobody was around, he pressed his ear against the door. Then he murmured beneath his breath, "They're both inside. I suggest you go now, in case he decides to leave early."

Aisha's mouse head was peering out of Horatio's pocket, as though she wanted to come too. But she would have to stay, safe in the folds of his robe.

"Okay," I breathed. "I'm going in."

I sank through the door and arrived outside the chamber from which emanated voices: those of Cyrus and a woman. Passing through this door too, I entered a lavish bedchamber. Another strikingly beautiful, tan-skinned jinni, her head bedecked with a tiara, her body sparkling with gems, sat on the edge of the four-poster bed while Cyrus stalked up and down the room. They were deep in conversation.

"Can you really be sure that she will be the one?" the queen asked Cyrus.

"I believe it from the very core of me," Cyrus replied. He stopped his prowling and sat down next to her on the bed, slipping an arm around her small waist. "Besides, if not her, then who?"

The queen shrugged. "I suppose, since there have been so many false starts along the way, I find it hard to have faith anymore."

Cyrus' large hand reached up to her face and stroked her forehead, moving up into the roots of her hair. "Yes, there have been," he replied softly. "And it is regrettable. If I'd had Nuriya from the start, I'm sure none of their lives would've been lost."

Whose lives?

"Even if my gut feeling turns out to be inaccurate," he went on, "what have I to lose? You have never expressed your fondness for Nuriya anyway, have you, my love?"

The queen stiffened. "I can't say that I have," she murmured, pursing her lips. "And I honestly don't see what attraction you have to her either."

Cyrus chuckled. He caught her chin and tilted her face upward, kissing her lips. "Attraction is a strange thing," he said, as he drew away. "But you should well understand the real reason I am drawn to her."

She nodded curtly, then as Cyrus continued lavishing affection on her—pulling her closer to him and showering kisses down her neck—she loosened a little. She reached for his hands and held them, creating a distance between them so she could look him in the eye. "I do agree with you, Cyrus, despite my reservations. If there's any way that she could be the one to give you the heirs you need, you must try it. As you say, the only loss would be Nuriya's life, which isn't even a loss at all."

Her previously stony face burst out into a smirk. Cyrus also grinned.

"I'm glad we're of one mind, my love." He pushed her back against the mattress and crawled over her, their kisses becoming more heated. She let out a soft moan as his hands travelled down her waist and then, for the first time ever, I saw it. The bottom half of a jinni. The mist that had covered the queen from the waist down, relinquished to reveal... quite an ordinary pair of legs. She wore a silk skirt around her waist—a garment that Cyrus quickly removed, revealing satin underwear.

That I didn't yell in horror at what happened next was a miracle.

Cyrus' mist also disappeared, giving way to the lower half of a scorpion.

His smooth, ebony torso flowed into a shiny black abdomen that segmented in several places. Eight black, pointed legs propped him up, and shooting out of his backside was a thick stinger with a razor-sharp, red-tinged tip.

What. The. Hell.

I'd read about a "King Scorpion" in an Egyptology class at school; a historical figure during the Protodynastic Period of Upper Egypt. *This guy sure takes that name to new levels of meaning.*

I was glad that I did not have Lucas with me, for I was sure he would have gasped out loud.

The half jinni, half scorpion scuttled leaned to his wife on the bed, and she stood up so that her face could be level with his.

I sensed that this scene was about to get a lot more disgusting as his hands lowered to her hips, but then she whispered, "I wish I could have you again." From the fire blazing in her eyes, she could mean only one thing by that.

"I know, my love," he breathed, even as he caressed her collarbone with his full lips. "But you did have me. We had children together. Just because our intimacy has lessened since I came to the throne does not mean that you have lost me. I still love you, just as I love your sister-in-law."

"And more than you loved your previous seven wives, I

hope." She said the words with a teasing smile. "And Nuriya," she added spitefully.

"Naturally," he murmured, breathing into her neck. "Otherwise you would not still be here, would you?"

The two continued embracing and it was clear as the minutes passed that, as impassioned as their kisses were, they were not going to go beyond second base... *Thank God.*

Now I realized why, even in the presence of all those harem ladies, Cyrus had kept his pants on... so to speak. And man. With an ass like that, I couldn't blame him. It was ironic—as surrounded by women as he was, he could not experience the pleasure that even a beggar could.

My mind continued to turn over, reverting to Hortencia's story. When he'd disappeared those four days before the contest to win the throne, had it been for this? He somehow managed to turn himself into this? Half scorpion? And was that why, in the arena, the scorpion had made no attempt to attack him? And why he had been able to stomach the poison so easily when his brother could not?

But how? How had he been able to turn himself into such a—I recalled Horatio's words booming through the court just a few hours ago—an abomination?

Whatever the case, Hortencia sure hadn't been joking. *"Everyone has something to hide."*

Some more than others...

BEN

My brain was exploding with so many questions, I was almost tempted to leave right now and return to Horatio to get some answers. But I stayed watching until Cyrus made a move to leave.

Then I darted out of the apartment and emerged in the corridor. Horatio had drifted further up the hallway, leaning against a wall, one hand planted over his right pocket.

"Horatio," I whispered hoarsely as I approached.

He led me to another apartment—apparently his own apartment this time—and into a sitting room, where he closed the door behind us. Solidifying myself, I wasn't even sure which of my hundred questions to ask first.

Aisha crawled out of Horatio's pocket and resumed her jinni form. "What happened?" she asked tensely, her eyes wide.

I was still quite speechless as to how to even describe the monstrosity I'd just witnessed.

Horatio eyed me darkly.

"He's..." I swallowed. "A scorpion mutant. H-half scorpion."

Aisha's jaw hit the floor. "*What?*"

"How is it possible?" I asked Horatio.

He shrugged. "I am certain of when it happened, but not how. Just before his coronation, before the test that his father set for him and his brother."

"He... he metamorphosed," Aisha gasped.

"Yes," Horatio said. "Permanently."

"How could he have done it?" Aisha asked, repeating my question.

"I doubt anybody knows how he actually pulled it off," Horatio replied. Noticing my bewildered expression, he added for my sake, "As I'm sure you are aware, jinn can morph themselves into various forms—be they animals or humanoids. But these are only temporary manifestations; jinn must always return to their original forms sooner or later... but not in the case of my father. I'm not sure that he could turn back even if he wanted to."

"And what exactly does he want Nuriya for?" I asked, recalling the king and queen's conversation.

Horatio's eyes darted toward Aisha's fearful face. He heaved a sigh before continuing to answer me in a low tone. "All the children my father has—me and all my siblings— were begotten before his coronation... as you may imagine, given his mutation. But he is not satisfied with us alone. He has been trying to have children since. It's tradition among the Drizans that each new generation must be more powerful than the last—the bar must be raised higher and higher to ensure that we remain the undisputed leaders of The Dunes. Since his turning into a monster, he's wished to create progeny just like him: toughened, robust... poisonous. He believes that this is the true way forward for our race. But in order to create such heirs, he is in need of a female jinni who is capable of adopting the same, permanent form as his. She must become half scorpion. My father believes that Nuriya is the female destined for this."

My fear for Nuriya increased tenfold, and Aisha looked like she was about to pass out.

"W-why would he believe that?" Aisha stammered.

"She is of impeccable lineage," Horatio said. "The Nasiris are renowned for their intolerance of inbreeding, and as she is the youngest of the Nasiri king's daughters, he believed— and still believes—that if any female is capable of surviving the turning and bearing his young, it is she… Hence, when he discovered that she was in love with another man, you can imagine his fury."

"He told you all this?" I asked, frowning.

Horatio shook his head, scoffing. "Never. The only two still living—apart from me—who have seen his scorpion half are my mother and stepmother; but that in itself is nothing unusual, if you know anything about jinn culture… I only discovered his secret after walking in on him and my mother unexpectedly one day. Even then, after I'd seen him, he made me swear secrecy and refrain from telling any of my siblings. He refused to give me any kind of explanation. Bit by bit, however, I managed to wear my mother down until she caved in and revealed to me more history."

"H-how would he turn Nuriya?" Aisha stammered.

"As I said," Horatio replied, "I do not know how he metamorphosed himself, let alone how he would inflict it on others. But whatever the method, he has tried it on his first seven wives… none of whom survived."

"And… he never tried it on your mother? Or the queen he was with just now?" I asked.

Horatio shook his head. "No. Nenia, whom you saw just now, is his eighth wife, while my mother is his ninth… and sworn last. Though his word means nothing."

"Why did he never try it with them?" I asked.

"Because after seven lost wives, he'd had enough experience to know that they wouldn't be successful either, especially since they hailed from the same bloodline as a previous wife who died."

Ugh. So he married, like, women who were sisters or cousins?

"Then of course," Horatio went on, "the dragons showed up offering the whereabouts of Nuriya. I'd never seen my father so happy as that day… and now he is preparing to wed her before beginning the mutation."

My head spun. This was all turning out to be far more complex than I had hoped. In spite of still being in shock, I could not lose awareness of our rapidly escaping time.

I rubbed my face with my hands, taking in a deep breath and trying to calm my brain. I looked up again and addressed Horatio. "You said before that what you would reveal to me was the key to freeing the Nasiris without killing Cyrus. How?" I couldn't understand how what I'd just witnessed could be considered a weakness. If anything, it just made the obstacle ahead of us seem even more impossible.

Horatio took a seat opposite me, resting his elbows on his knees and looking at me intently. "I believe that his transformation is the cause of his unparalleled powers. How else could a single jinni uphold a bond over all the Nasiris at once—who are certainly not considered a weak clan by any stretch?" He shifted his gaze to Aisha, then back to me.

"Besides that, since discovering his secret, I have observed him as much as possible without arousing suspicion. I visited his apartment at odd times, most times watching without him even knowing. I have noticed that he has a ritual of drinking a bright orangey-red liquid... liquid that's almost the exact color of the tip of his stinger."

Aisha and I stared at him, wondering exactly what he was implying. Aisha voiced where my thoughts were turning before I could. "Y-you think he's drinking... his own venom?"

Horatio nodded slowly, grimacing. "I don't know where else he'd get it from."

That was a visual I did not need. *God. Can this story get any more gross?*

"He drinks it like a ritual, morning, afternoon and evening, and he keeps a stash of it in his kitchen," Horatio continued.

"I've seen him drink it too," I murmured. "And he's feeding it to Nuriya."

"Ugh!" Aisha cried.

"So you've already done your own share of spying?" Horatio said to me.

I nodded.

Horatio's nose curled in distaste. "Then apparently, she has already proven that she can withstand the poison... In any case, flooding his veins with venom must be key to his strength, otherwise he would never drink the vile stuff so religiously—and it is vile, believe me. I've smelt it," he added in an undertone. "Since the poison originates in his tail, that would seem the logical place to target, if he was caught in his physical form, his *full* physical form. Damaging it somehow, maybe even depleting its stock of poison, might severely weaken him. At least, enough for the Nasiris to use their own powers to break free from his bond."

A span of silence followed.

"So," Aisha began, her voice unsteady, "how and when would we get him in his physical state, his *full* physical state?"

"It would have to be during one of his visits to his wives. He isn't scheduled for another one until the day after tomorrow—my mother."

The day after tomorrow. I cursed beneath my breath.

"We cannot wait that long," Aisha voiced for me, glancing at me nervously. "It has to be tonight."

"Tonight?" The doubt in Horatio's eyes made my stomach clench. He stood up and began pacing up and down, slowly, thoughtfully. "In that case... I might have another idea. It could kill us all, but it's an idea nonetheless."

I held my breath, waiting for him to continue.

"However, we could not do it without Nuriya's help."

I raised a brow in question.

"On the night of the wedding, it's tradition for husband and wife to reveal each other fully to themselves," Horatio explained to me. "It's also the same night that—according to my mother—he has historically attempted the mutation... But I'm guessing that they would have some time alone first."

"We'd have to catch him before that." Aisha shuddered.

"I've no idea if this will work. Usually royal weddings are planned many weeks in advance, and I'm not sure my father would want to rush his wedding with Nuriya, considering what a landmark he considers it to be. I can't help but think he'd want everything polished to perfection. However, if the request came from Nuriya... you just never know. In any case, we could try."

"Try to get Nuriya to convince Cyrus to hold the wedding tonight?" Aisha's brows raised so high they almost disappeared into her hairline.

"As I said," Horatio muttered, "it's a long shot. It's up to you whether you want to take the risk."

"We'll take the risk," I answered immediately.

Risk wasn't something that scared me anymore. Failure was.

BEN

So we need Nuriya's help. Last time I'd seen the woman, she'd looked so far gone, she could hardly help herself. And even if we managed to convince Nuriya to try to shift the wedding to tonight—which was preposterously short notice by anyone's measure—and Cyrus agreed, I still wasn't sure what Horatio was thinking. How would we even overpower his father in order to damage his stinger? But one step at a time. *No point counting eggs before they've hatched...*

It was decided that I would go to Nuriya and attempt the persuasion. First, as a fae, I was capable of being invisible to jinn, and second, I should be at no disadvantage compared to Aisha because Nuriya was fond of me... at least the old

Nuriya had been. I was not sure what state of mind she was in now. Hopefully she would still recognize me.

I left Horatio and Aisha in his apartment and hurried back to Cyrus' quarters. A place I had hoped I would not need to return to. Horatio had instructed me to go fast, for if I hurried, I would have about half an hour with Nuriya before Cyrus returned. Apparently the king and queen had made it a habit to go for a leisurely wander in the desert after one of their rendezvous.

As I raced along, I prayed that Cyrus would keep to his schedule.

I entered the apartment, moving from room to room until I found Nuriya, slumped in a ruby-studded rocking chair. A book lay open in her shackled hands, but she was not reading it. She was gazing absentmindedly at the opposite wall, her face devoid of expression.

Still invisible to her, I moved in front of her and crouched down before solidifying myself. As my face appeared before hers, life sparked in her eyes and she jerked backward in shock, the book falling from her palms.

Well at least she's conscious.

Then to my relief, she gasped my name. "Benjamin?"

She's not as far gone as I feared.

Before she could protest, I grabbed her hands and led her toward where I remembered the nearest bathroom was located. Pulling her inside, I bolted the door behind us. She was still gaping at me, her mouth opening and closing like a fish's.

"How... What..." she stammered, making too much noise for comfort. I placed my palm over her mouth and shushed her.

"Nuriya," I whispered, even as my ears strained to remain aware of any sounds in the apartment. I could only imagine what Cyrus would do if he found me holed up in his bathroom with his betrothed. "Is there anyone else in this apartment right now?" I demanded.

"I'm not sure," she breathed. "There were some servants who came in earlier, but they may have exited now.... What are you doing here?" She frowned so hard a deep line formed down the center of her forehead.

"I've come to free you and your family," I said.

At this, she broke down. "Benjamin. Oh, Benjamin!" She flung her arms around me and held me tight, filling me with a sense of déjà vu. She clung to me like I was her lost son, as she'd done to me several times back in The Oasis. When I managed to detach myself from her, tears were streaming down her cheeks. "You came for me. You came for us!"

"Yes, but hush!"

"How will you help us escape?" she stammered, fighting to lower her hysterical voice.

"Before I can do anything, I need your help," I said.

She clutched my hands. "What?"

I felt a stab of guilt for what I was about to request of her. "Whatever it takes," I began, "you need to make your wedding to Cyrus happen tonight."

Her lips parted in shock. "What? Why?"

"I don't have time to answer questions now," I said. "You must just do what I say."

Another twinge of guilt.

The jinni's eyes filled with fear, and that was without her knowing what fate lay in wait for her after the wedding. But I couldn't tell her. Not if I wanted to stand any chance of getting the Nasiris out of here and meeting the fae on the mountainside on time.

She drew in a breath. "Okay… How do I do that?"

"I'm not sure. You have to figure it out. Do anything. But don't fail. Fixing the wedding is all you have to do; I will take care of the rest."

"All right," she said. "I will try. I swear, I will try."

"No," I said, more forcefully than I had intended, even as I found myself speaking the same words the oracle had spoken to me in my time of despair. "Not try. Trying is for cowards."

Nuriya pursed her lips, stiffening. Determination flickered in her golden eyes. "You're right. Not try. I *will*."

BEN

I left Nuriya in the bathroom, where she said she would immediately take a shower and get ready, while I drifted to the entrance hall of the apartment. Here I sat down in a corner in my subtle form and waited until Cyrus returned home. He appeared to be in a good mood as he drifted through to the bedroom, calling Nuriya's name.

Nuriya emerged through a doorway, looking like a new person. The hope I'd given her seemed to have sparked life in her, and even Cyrus appeared stunned. Her eyes had regained their sparkle, and she looked as striking as ever, long black hair flowing down her shoulders, wearing a silky low-cut dress that hugged her curvaceous body. She brought a heady scent of jasmine with her into the bedroom.

"Yes," she said, her lips curving in a smile, revealing her white teeth.

Regaining composure, Cyrus closed the distance between them, cupping her face in his hands. He took her in with admiration before stooping down to close his lips around hers.

"Beauty," he murmured. His hands settled on her waist and his gaze raked hungrily over the rest of her body, like he was undressing her with his eyes.

"You are looking different this afternoon," he remarked, taking her hand and pulling her toward the bed.

"I... feel different," she said, following him. Her voice was surprisingly steady for someone who had been a trembling wreck less than an hour ago.

"Why is that?" Cyrus wondered.

"Today I... I realized how much I miss you when you're gone." As the two sank down on the mattress, she reached out and stroked his cheek timidly with her fingers. "And I realized that... I'm unhappy without you."

She leaned in and this time kissed his lips. From the pleasant surprise that crossed Cyrus' face, I was sure that was the first time she had ever done that to him willingly. He pushed her back on the mattress and lay beside her, his arms snaking around her and locking her flush against him. I felt quite amazed that he seemed to actually believe her words. After everything he'd done to her, I thought he'd be suspicious at this change of mood. I could only assume that, when it came to women, his ego was bigger than his brain.

Watching them make out for the next few minutes was sickening, knowing how much Nuriya must be despising every second. But she was putting on a good act. By the time Cyrus surfaced again, he was quite breathless, blood rising to his lips.

Nuriya, still lying on her side, propped her head up with her elbow and traced her right hand down his muscled chest. "I was also thinking that... that maybe we could make the wedding sooner."

Cyrus' eyes lit up. His face broke out in a wide smile. "Of course," he said. "If that's what you wish. We shall have it within a week! Never mind all the extra luxury and rituals we'd have time to plan by waiting longer. I'm not so concerned with any of it as I am with seeing you... all of you... for the first time." His eyes glistened with lust.

I couldn't miss the gulp in Nuriya's throat, but it seemed that Cyrus was too preoccupied to notice.

"I was thinking even sooner," Nuriya said sweetly.

Cyrus stared at her. "Sooner than a week?"

"Yes," she said, and then she averted her eyes, playing bashful.

"How soon?" he pressed, clearly enjoying himself immensely.

She pressed her lips against his again in a deep, long kiss before whispering, "Tonight."

"Tonight?" Cyrus actually laughed. "Well, if that is what the love of my life wishes, then... It shall be done." He kissed her again before leaving her side and gliding out of bed.

"Then we have only hours to prepare. It will not be the grandest wedding by far... but believe me, Nuriya, it will be the truest." His eyes lingered on her adoringly, and I found myself wondering whether there was indeed a part of him that loved her. Just not a large enough part to stop him from destroying her life...

"I will leave to begin preparations at once!" he announced, already moving toward the door. "And I will send some servants up to help you dress."

With that, he hurried out of the room.

As Nuriya gazed after him, I could see the fear rising up behind her eyes.

Poor woman. She looked like a lamb. A lamb ready for slaughter.

BEN

Once Cyrus was safely gone, I solidified myself before Nuriya. I promised her that all would be okay—even though it was a promise I didn't even know that we could keep. I told her to go along with everything, keep playing the part, and that I would come for her. She nodded, and it killed me to see how much faith she placed in me.

Then I had to leave, almost bumping into a group of servants entering through the door on my way out. I hurried along the palace corridors back to Horatio's apartment. When I returned to the sitting room where I had left them, Horatio and Aisha were still sitting here, close to each other and deep in conversation.

Their eyes shot toward me. I hurriedly explained to them that I had been successful in getting through to Nuriya, and that Cyrus had agreed to make the wedding this evening.

As if to make my point, a loud bell began to ring outside. Then came a voice, booming through the very walls of the palace:

"Royal wedding in five hours! King Cyrus will wed his beloved Nuriya!"

I swallowed hard.

Aisha swallowed harder.

***

Tonight. Everything hung on tonight. If this failed—for one or more of the many reasons that it could and should fail— then that would be it. Sherus would come after me, Lucas, Kailyn and the other three Underworld escapees... We had to pull this off. We just had to.

I waited tensely with Horatio and Aisha during the hours before the wedding as we continued to discuss our harebrained scheme. It felt like the more we discussed it, the more holes we saw in it, until our conversation ended up petering out. We'd discussed what we could. Now all that was left was to do it.

About half an hour before the wedding was due to start, I left for the grand court, where Horatio had told me the wedding would take place, while Horatio headed in the opposite direction, Aisha the mouse in his pocket. We had agreed that he would take Aisha back to the desert, and she would return to Lake Nasser where my family and the dragons awaited. There she would fetch the dragons, who were due to play a part in our plan later this evening... assuming they agreed. If the shifters did, they would be essentially striking out any goodwill that the dragons and the Drizans had accumulated over God knew how many years. Though it didn't seem like they had many favors left anyway, so they hopefully wouldn't be much worse off.

I refocused my attention on my surroundings. I had not passed down these corridors at such a busy time before. And although I knew that jinn could not see fae in their subtle forms, it was still disconcerting to be so close to them. I went slowly, much slower than I would've liked. There was a long line outside the great court; it looked like the whole palace was piling in. I followed, managing to find a gap to slip through and enter the chamber.

It was so packed, the huge chamber seemed small suddenly, and all the wedding attendees were dressed to the nines. In spite of only having five hours to prepare, the court was gorgeously decorated with garlands of vibrant flowers hugging the columns and silken orange streamers trailing from the ceiling. It was like a scene from heaven... except for Nuriya, who I had just spotted in one corner surrounded by a group of maids. I was sure that this place could not look more hellish to her. My eyes swept past a screen fixed in the center of the other side of the court, where I spotted Cyrus with a group of male jinn.

Then I glimpsed Horatio passing through the entrance. He scanned the room and then moved farther back in the crowd, clearly trying to attract as little attention to himself as possible. But he didn't get far. What appeared to be one of his older sisters approached him and pulled him to the front row.

The wedding ceremony started promptly on the hour. By now, the room was packed to the brim.

The screen was removed by a jinni in the garb of a priest—an austere brown robe and shaven head—allowing the beaming groom and slightly trembling bride to see each other. Closing the distance between them, they met in the center.

The priest began reciting chants from an ancient book he had manifested out of thin air—chants consisting of words I could not understand. This went on for an uncomfortably long time. I looked around, wondering if anybody else was getting bored or antsy, but it appeared that I was the only one—I and most likely Horatio. Everyone else was leaning forward with rapt attention, eyes glued to the bride and groom.

Finally the priest finished his recitation, and now I was expecting the couple to exchange vows of some sort, but they didn't. Apparently that wasn't done in jinn weddings. Instead they immediately exchanged rings—fat golden rings studded with an obnoxious array of gems—and then Cyrus pulled Nuriya against him and kissed her full on the mouth.

Then, to my surprise, Cyrus removed Nuriya's chains. There were murmurings in the crowd. He cast his eyes over everyone, a broad smile on his face. "As husband and wife, we are now bound more tightly than ever before." He cast her golden manacles aside, sending them clanging to the floor. Nuriya rubbed her wrists, looking only half-relieved.

And then with a clap of his hands, the priest announced the marriage complete. I suspected that since this was so last-minute, they had kept the formalities to the minimum. I guessed this wedding would have been a lot more elaborate and long-winded if it had taken place in a month, or whenever Cyrus had been planning to hold it.

Cheers erupted, echoing deafeningly around the court. And then began the festivities. Platter upon platter of food fit for an emperor, troupes of musicians, dancing girls, and enough liquor to fill a lake. Either jinn were terrible at holding down alcohol, or this stuff was strong, because after barely an hour had passed, I could not spot a single jinni who was not blind drunk... except for Horatio, Nuriya and, to my dismay, Cyrus.

Finally, as I was beginning to grow desperate, Cyrus took his new wife by the waist and bade goodbye to the drunk partygoers. He drifted with her toward the exit. I caught Horatio's eyes following them, too. Hurrying after Cyrus and Nuriya, I couldn't afford to lose sight of them.

As I moved along the hallways, keeping a distance of several feet between me and the newlyweds, I thought of Horatio and what he was supposed to do now—alert Aisha and the dragons that the wedding had finished. But he had to do it fast, because I needed him back here.

Cyrus headed straight back to his apartment as Horatio had predicted. Guiding Nuriya inside, he led her to the bedroom and seated her on the bed. He kissed her neck, his lips trailing down her throat to her bosom. Then he unraveled her silken gown until she was stripped to her undergarments. It looked like every muscle in her body was tensed, though from this angle, I could not see her face. I could only imagine how difficult it was for her to keep up this act while having no idea if I would even come through on my promise. *I can't let her down.*

Cyrus, his bottom half still covered in mist, ran his palms down Nuriya's torso, stopping just above her navel. Then he whispered in a husky voice, "We are wed now. Reveal yourself, my love."

Her breath hitched, but slowly, obediently, Nuriya's lower half emerged. Cyrus ran his wide palms down her slender legs and explored them for a while before returning to look upon her face. He removed the silk cloth draped around his chest, and then the heavy pendant from his neck, tossing them aside on the mattress. He raised a brow, a small smile quirking his lips. "Now," he said. "Would you like to see me?"

God, no. Not again.

And yet our entire plan was depending on his scorpion butt making another appearance.

"Yes," Nuriya murmured.

I held my breath, waiting for him to transform and for my eyeballs to be once again assaulted, but instead he scooped her up in his arms and shifted her off the bed, remaining in his smokey form. Then he moved around the bed and, with one powerful thrust of his arms, sent it sliding across the floor to the other side of the room. Where the bed had been, cut into the floor, was… a trapdoor. A secret trapdoor.

Nuriya eyed it uncertainly.

"I wish to take you somewhere first," Cyrus explained.

"Where?" Nuriya asked, no longer hiding the fear in her voice.

"Follow and you shall see, my love." Taking her hand, he

pulled her to the trapdoor. He stooped down and creaked open the door, and then, picking her up again, descended into the hole.

Where is Horatio? I felt leery going down without him. He was supposed to be here by now. In any case, it was hard to miss that hole in the floor. He would know where we had gone.

I approached the trapdoor and gazed down to see the two of them disappearing into gloom. As I hurried down, there was a strange musky smell. Reaching the bottom, I found myself emerging in a dank dungeon, lit by torches. The walls were bare—made of stone—except for the far wall, which was covered entirely by a long red curtain. There wasn't anything polished about the place except for another luxurious bed, identical to the one upstairs, placed in the center.

Nuriya gazed around. *A rather strange place to bring a bride on her wedding night.*

"What is this?" Nuriya asked.

Cyrus hushed her.

The firelight danced across Nuriya's face. Her forehead had broken out in a sweat. I could practically hear the question running through her mind: *Where's Benjamin?*

I wished I could somehow let her know that I was right here, just waiting...

Finally, it happened. After laying her down on the bed, he propped himself up on the mattress and the bottom half of him slowly manifested.

Her eyes bulging in her sockets, Nuriya screamed.

Way to kill the moment.

Cyrus appeared displeased by this, to say the least. *How dare Nuriya not be delighted to discover she'd just married a scorpion mutant!*

She scrambled off the bed and bolted for the door, but Cyrus' eight legs caught up with her too fast. He grabbed hold of her and gathered her in a crushing hold before dragging her back to the bed. Apparently she was incapable of escaping by vanishing herself.

"It's all right," he said, taking a deep breath—as if to calm his own annoyance as much as Nuriya's fear. "It's me. Just me," he whispered, leaning down to catch her trembling lips in his. "And you'll come to love me for what I am… as well as for what you will become."

Now was the time to strike. Now, or it might be never. My eyes shot toward the stairwell. I hoped to see Horatio, who was supposed to come equipped with weapons for me, but still he wasn't there. *Where the hell is he?*

My eyes raked over the chamber for any kind of weapon that I could use, but all I spotted were the burning torches. I moved for the nearest one to me, but before I reached it,

Cyrus darted with Nuriya toward the other side of the room and stopped in front of the long red curtain. He drew it open. I froze.

The curtain had been covering the entrance to another torchlit chamber, much like the one I stood in now. Except in the center was a pool of bright orange liquid, and behind the pool, crouched in the shadows, loomed the dark outline of... a black scorpion. A real, full-bodied scorpion. A scorpion larger than a horse. Its tiny eyes gleamed as they turned in their sockets, and its orange-red tipped stinger— the same color as Cyrus'—rose above its head.

If my sister had been here to see this creeper, she would have had a heart attack. Poor Nuriya certainly looked close to it.

The liquid in the pool, however, was almost more disconcerting than the scorpion itself. It looked identical to what I'd seen Cyrus drinking. Perhaps he had not been drinking his own venom after all... In which case, would damaging his stinger even help? Would we need to target both Cyrus and the scorpion?

"Meet the queen of scorpions," Cyrus announced, proudly gesturing toward the creature. "The very first scorpion ever to be captured by my great-great-grandfather."

"H-how?" Nuriya gasped, close to hyperventilating.

"My uncle used to tell me tales as a boy of the exploits of

my great ancestor. One of the stories involved his creating this beauty, Neema." He cast another loving glance at his pet.

He should hook up with her instead.

"Nobody believed that she could still be alive, after all that time, even after being freed from captivity and released into the wild. They underestimated just how potent a breed my great-great-grandfather had created. I, on the other hand, did believe... I hunted her down and found her."

He scuttled with Nuriya closer to the venomous pool. "You know," he said thoughtfully, running his palms down Nuriya's back, "Neema's venom is so powerful, it is infectious to certain species... transformative, even. A gentle dip in a pool of her poison can sometimes even mutate shapeshifting species of our kind permanently. It merely depends on how strong the bather is."

Nuriya's breath hitched and she struggled once again to break free.

"I was lucky to be born from a strong bloodline," he went on, "just as you are lucky."

I couldn't wait any longer. Shooting for a torch, the only thing in this chamber I could possibly use as a weapon, I spotted Horatio in the stairwell. *Finally*. He was half translucent, and to my relief, he had brought half a dozen swords.

I rushed over and grabbed a blade from him, forced to assume a solid state.

Nuriya's scream pierced the chamber.

When I whirled around, it was to see Cyrus bending over the pool, holding Nuriya's head under. Cursing beneath my breath, I raced over to him, raising the sword and aiming it at the base of his stinger. But before I reached four feet from him—even though I made no sound—he spun around abruptly, as if he had eyes at the back of his head.

With him no longer pushing Nuriya's head down, she spluttered and fought to pull herself out of the pool, even as she cried in agony, as if the venom burned her skin.

Cyrus took me in, his dark eyes narrowing. "Fae?" he breathed.

Before I could react, a chorus of mighty roars blasted overhead, so loud they seemed to shake the very foundations of the palace. The roar of dragons. They had arrived to distract the rest of the jinn.

Cyrus scowled, then lunged for me with supernatural speed. I managed to vanish myself just in time, forced to drop my sword in the process.

"Come out, come out wherever you are." Cyrus' voice echoed eerily around the dungeon.

I backed into one corner, looking toward the stairwell where I glimpsed Horatio hiding behind the door. An idea occurring to me, I resumed my solid state and shot toward the exit. As Cyrus followed through the door, I had to hope that Horatio would be courageous enough to strike him as he passed by in my wake.

Horatio did attempt it, holding a sword in the air, but he only became another victim of Cyrus' uncanny sense of awareness.

Cyrus discovered him behind the door too soon. He stood gaping at his son, stunned... and hurt.

"Horatio?" he said, his voice hoarse.

Horatio's gaze was steely as he looked back at his formidable father. His mouth grim, his expression resolute, Horatio said, "I've had enough."

Cyrus just stared, as though he simply could not accept that his son had sided with a fae in a plot against him. Then anger lined his face. His arms shot out and although Horatio tried to dodge, Cyrus grabbed his throat as easily as a child would a doll. Cyrus slammed him against the wall, his hold around his neck tightening.

As much as I wanted to help Horatio, I couldn't. Taking advantage of Cyrus' shock and devastation over his son, I thinned myself and soared back into the dungeon. To my horror, Nuriya was no longer trembling or spluttering. She lay still. Quite still. *Don't be dead, Nuriya. Don't be dead.* Could the venom really have killed her already? She'd only been held under for a few seconds. I checked her pulse. She was still alive. For how long, there was no saying.

Another round of roars rumbled through the palace, followed by what must have been floods of fire.

Neema snapped her pincers, agitated. Uncurling her legs, she began to creep forward. *I really don't need to deal with that too...*

I hurried to scoop up Nuriya in my arms, even as the venom she was coated with stung my own skin. Cyrus yelled his son's name. I turned to see Horatio speeding into the room, having somehow slipped from his father's grasp. Not for long. Cyrus came zooming into the room and made a beeline for him. But then, on noticing me, he stopped midway.

I was forced to thin myself again, leaving Nuriya on the ground, as he lunged for me. I hurried over to Horatio's end as Cyrus crossed the room and rolled Nuriya back into the pool.

She's unconscious. If the venom doesn't finish her off first, won't she drown?

Despite her "superior bloodline", she wasn't showing any signs of being able to handle the poison any better than Cyrus' previous wives. I wondered what made Cyrus think that she would still turn, or perhaps he didn't and was just happy to let her die.

"We should try to damage both of them," Horatio mouthed, sensing my approach. "Both of their stingers."

How?

I didn't need to ask the question. It was clear that he did not know how, any more than I knew, or he would have clarified. To make matters worse, Cyrus had just vanished his lower half and replaced it with his usual trail of reddish mist.

Oh, God. We've missed our chance.

We'd spent so much time waiting for him to revert to his scorpion form. All of it now wasted.

How are we ever going to pull this off?

Before I could sink into a state of mind the oracle would greatly disapprove of, I instead focused my thoughts on action.

My eyes shot to Cyrus as he lunged forward, approaching Horatio again. Taking advantage of the distraction, I swept across the chamber toward one of the swords Horatio had dropped. Forced to solidify in order to scoop it up, I wrapped my fingers around the hilt before darting into the second chamber. I wanted to dive into the pool and collect Nuriya, but I could only pick one objective. Trying to fish Nuriya out would attract Cyrus' attention again, and he would only dump her back into the pool... but if I could damage his scorpion pet...

I soared over and passed the pool, arriving a few feet from the scorpion.

As I maneuvered around the animal, I saw that she was chained to the wall. I was about to attempt to leap up onto her back to get closer to her stinger when a powerful force collided with my back, winding me and knocking the blade from my hands. Weakened, I fell to the ground, almost in the reach of the scorpion's pincers.

Cyrus loomed over me. I could not see where Horatio was. If he was even still alive. Cyrus' hand shot down and gripped my head, his powerful fingers raking into my hair, and he forced my neck to the side in such a violent motion I was surprised that it did not snap. I had to remind myself that I was not a vampire anymore. Fae, when in their physical state, could be damaged just like humans could. I struggled to thin myself, but couldn't. I could only assume it was because Cyrus was already holding me.

Firelight glistened in Cyrus' gold-plated teeth as a sinister smile split his face.

"You wanted to get a closer look at her, did you?"

He dragged me closer to the scorpion. His hands felt like iron as he gripped my shoulders and turned me to face his pet. The beast was thoroughly agitated by now, pulling against her restraints and snapping her sharp pincers.

"Neema does not get visitors very often," Cyrus said,

looking at her affectionately. "Sweet thing. Look at how excited she is."

He lowered me until my body was a foot away from her pincers and jaws that looked like a meat grinder. Forcing me closer still, Cyrus laughed as the scorpion clamped her pincers around my arms, their sharp edges digging painfully into my flesh. I moved to kick her, but all that did was infuriate her further.

No. I did not go through all of this to end up as scorpion food.

"Stop!" a voice roared. Horatio's voice.

His form whizzed past me and hurtled into his father, causing Cyrus to stagger back, and in the process, pulling me away with him. I grunted as the pincers ripped through my skin.

Cyrus sent Horatio crashing against the wall, sending a bracket of burning torches crashing to the floor. Then he dragged me to Neema again.

"We couldn't deprive Neema of her meal now," Cyrus drawled. "That would be terribly unfair."

As he lowered me again, I caught sight of one of the torches that had rolled just nearby. In a burst of desperation, I lunged for it and managed to reach out with my arm and grab the torch. I swung it up toward Cyrus' face. He released his grip in shock. Then I swiped the torch against the scorpion, who screeched and scuttled backward.

This torch had only bought me a few seconds. I had two choices: flee, or try to finish off what Horatio and I had started. But fleeing wasn't an option for me. *Fleeing the jinn only to be thrust back into The Underworld.*

I was on the verge of shooting to the other side of the chamber, where more swords lay, when a spark of fire fell from my torch to my feet. In all the commotion, the tip of the torch had loosened.

I was expecting to feel an intense burning, and my skin to singe. Instead my feet caught on fire. Then the flames spread within seconds to the rest of my body, licking up my torso as though I was doused in gasoline, until there wasn't an inch of me that wasn't covered in flames. Still, I felt no pain. Just a warm, even comfortable, tingling sensation.

Was I just in too much pain for my brain to even register it? *What is happening to me?* As bewildered as I was, I didn't hesitate a second longer. Taking advantage of Cyrus' surprise, I lunged for the sword again and swept over the scorpion's back with all the supernatural speed I could muster. I wrapped my burning limbs around the stinger. My fire seared her body. A split second later, I'd hacked off the bulbous tip of the stinger. As it fell to the floor, I darted down with it and drove the blade through it, twisting and turning the weapon as the poison leaked out. The scorpion's screams were deafening, and so were Cyrus'. The intensity of their cries matched one another, as though it had been Cyrus' tail I'd chopped. The scorpion thrashed wildly as blood and venom leaked from her end. To my surprise, Cyrus' own lower body revealed itself, as though it was triggered by the pain. Though unlike Neema's, his stinger was still intact.

Fury shone in his eyes, brighter than the flames engulfing my body. He shot toward me and I tried to thin myself, but I couldn't. *This fire is keeping me in my physical state.* I gazed around the room for Horatio. Where he had been slumped on the floor was now an empty space. He was gone. *Where is he? Did he just abandon me? And Nuriya!* I thought with a wave of panic. She was still in the pool. God, I'd forgotten.

Before Cyrus grabbed me again, I reached out for another torch and swung it in Cyrus' direction. He didn't even bother to dodge this time. He whacked it out of my hands, sending it tumbling to the ground. He dragged me over to the pool and then, withdrawing a dagger from his belt, held it up against my neck.

His face twitched maniacally. "You will pay for this, fae."

As he brought the knife driving toward my chest, a wave of heat rolled through the chamber. Cyrus paused midair and twisted his head. A mass of fire—perhaps shot from a dragon?—was heading toward us with such speed, Cyrus didn't even have a chance to react as it slammed against him, forcing him to drop the knife and me. He fell to the floor, allowing me to rise to my feet, and as I did I found myself face to face with Lucas. *Also fathered by fire...* His whole body blazed, just like mine. He had been the flaming cannonball.

My eyes traveled past him quickly and I glimpsed Horatio and Aisha, holding more swords. *Horatio left me to get help.* As Cyrus scrambled to his feet—or legs—Horatio, Aisha and Lucas lunged at once, all three piling onto him.

Let's finish this once and for all...

Sweeping up my sword, I leapt onto Cyrus' back and struck just beneath his stinger's bulb, the same thin area where I'd struck Neema's body. Cyrus roared so loudly it felt like my ear drums would split. I twisted the knife deeper into the bright red bulb as it detached, mashing it up into a pulp. Poison oozed from it as though it were a seething boil.

It was a disgusting sight to behold, both the mother scorpion and her mutant writhing together on the ground.

"I-I think we've done enough damage," Horatio said, even as he looked petrified at what we'd just done. "Under this pain, I can't imagine he's strong enough to hold up the bond..."

"Let's go," Lucas said.

"No!" Aisha roared, before we could even consider leaving the dungeon. The next thing I knew, she'd wrapped her legs around Cyrus' waist and plunged her dagger right through his throat.

He choked, blood spurting everywhere. Aisha's sweaty face twisted with rage even as tears welled behind her eyes. "This is for my family." She jerked the knife lower down his throat, creating a sickeningly wide gash and causing more blood to pool. "For my brothers." She tore sideways. "My fathers." She withdrew the knife and made a puncture in the side of his throat. "And my uncles."

My stomach lurched as, with a sharp pivot of the blade, she tore Cyrus' head clean off.

It all happened so fast, Horatio, Lucas and I just gaped.

The mighty Cyrus Drizan. Dead. At the hands of Aisha.

BEN

It was Lucas who roused us to our senses. "We've got to leave," he breathed. Both his and my flames had died down by now.

"Wait!" I said, darting toward the pool. "Nuriya!"

"She's all right," Horatio said behind me, his voice shaky. "I-I took her out of there when m-my father's focus was on you."

Thank God. I couldn't believe that she would have been alive in there after all this time.

We rushed to the exit and up the stairwell, arriving back in Cyrus' bedroom.

"What happened?" I asked, looking around the empty apartment.

"We arrived as planned," Aisha said, her chest heaving, eyes still gleaming with menace. "We couldn't have picked a better night than the night of a royal wedding. Everyone's blind drunk, even the guards. We hardly even needed the dragons to cause a distraction."

"Who else came?" I asked anxiously.

"Everyone," Aisha replied. "Though only Lucas, the dragons and I came down to the palace. The rest are waiting up in the desert for us."

Good.

"And where's Nuriya?" I asked.

Horatio led us to a cupboard near the exit to Cyrus' apartment. When he drew it open, Nuriya lay there curled up in a ball. She was trembling, but thankfully conscious. Her face, covered in burns, lit up a little when she saw me and she even cracked a brief smile.

"I knew you'd come for me," she said to me.

Horatio picked her up, and then we all hurried away from the apartment.

"Now what?" I asked.

"Now the bond should, uh"—Horatio's voice cracked. He swallowed hard—"definitely be removed." I wondered if there was a part of him that grieved his father's death. Mostly he seemed to be in a state of shock.

"Which means we have to free the rest," I said.

"We already gathered them in anticipation of you killing Cyrus," Aisha said. "They're waiting as close to the exit as possible—in one of the entrance halls the dragons didn't scorch yet. At least... we gathered as many as we could." Aisha's tone dropped, then she choked up. "H-he killed..." She gulped. "He killed every man in our family."

Damn. I couldn't blame Aisha for charging at Cyrus the way she had.

She regained composure, clenching her thick jaw as she vanished us to the desert.

Indeed, a crowd was waiting there. My family, River and also a group of female jinn. It warmed me to see Safi among them. *Thank God we got them out of that mess.*

River leapt at me as I approached. I wrapped my arms around her waist and kissed her neck, breathing in her familiar scent.

"Are you all right?" my mother asked, as my parents and sister hurried to me.

"All right." I nodded. "Where are the dra—"

"It's not safe to stay here longer." I spun to see Jeriad approaching us at a run, our other dragon companions close behind him. "We must leave. Now."

I couldn't have agreed more.

We returned to the islet in Lake Nasser, and for the first time in hours, I was able to catch a breath. I dove into the lake, taking River with me. Dipping under with her, I relished the cool water against my skin.

The freed Nasiris remained speechless, shaken and traumatized by their time in the Drizans' palace. I wasn't sure what Horatio—the only male jinni among us—planned to do now. I wondered if his people would punish him if he returned. Whatever the case, he decided to tag along with us.

When we climbed out of the lake from our brief bath, we had to forge on to the mountains… where our real problems would begin.

BEN

Before leaving for Canada, I briefed the jinn about what was required of them—that I was indebted to a fae, and they needed to help me pay off this debt. Of course, I still wasn't able to tell them exactly what the fae wanted their assistance with, for I had no idea myself.

Although they were still in a daze, I was relieved that at least there was no resistance on their part. Aisha, having recovered a large part of her family, was less weak from mourning. Even though the others were worn, they all agreed to help me, including Nuriya.

And so together we left Lake Nasser—everyone except for the dragons. I told my family and River that they did not need to come with us, but they insisted. We traveled by the jinns' magic toward the mountain portal where I was due to meet Sherus in just a couple of hours' time. As we reached the peak and gazed down at its smooth snow-clad surface, we caught sight of a lone figure already waiting there. Sherus was early. Goosebumps ran along my skin, and I instinctively held River closer.

This is it.

As we touched down, my stomach clenched as he turned around to face us all. He raised a brow, as though surprised I'd kept my word. Then he moved closer, his brilliant amber eyes fixed on my jinn companions. He cleared his throat.

"I'm glad you came," he said.

I nodded curtly, then gestured toward the jinn on either side of me. "These jinn are willing to assist you in whatever your request is," I said. "Now would you please give a briefing on what exactly you need from them?"

"Naturally," Sherus said. "Come with me." He gestured toward the gaping portal.

The jinn exchanged uncertain glances with me before we moved forward. I shot a glance at the rest of our group—both vampire and fae—indicating that they stay, but since River was already on my back, and only tightened her grip on me at Sherus' invitation to follow, I let her stay as she was.

We drifted to the hole and sank inside. Sherus led us through the swirling walls of the tunnel. River filled my right ear with a soft gasp as we emerged in what looked like outer space. The endless, star-speckled void.

"Are you okay?" I whispered to River, suddenly anxious. For a moment I feared that perhaps the atmosphere might not be tolerable for non-subtle beings.

But she replied, "Yes. I'm okay."

She did not sound like she was suffocating, so I returned my attention to the fae.

"Take us closer to those stars," Sherus requested the jinn.

He was pointing to the brightest star in view, one that had caught my attention the last time I'd come down here. Obediently, the jinn used their powers to vanish us God knew how many miles closer. When we reached our destination I realized why Sherus had spoken in plural. The "star" I'd seen from a distance was actually four distinct, glowing globes, each with a different hue—white, green, blue, and golden-brown—and very close together. They were aligned in a gentle arc, like a bridge. A bridge of stars.

I looked back to Sherus. His expression was tinged with melancholy. He swallowed before beginning his much-needed explanation. "Those stars you see are the realms of the fae—fae of all elements."

"What do you mean by elements?"

"Earth, water, fire, and air," he said, pointing to each of the stars in succession: golden-brown for earth, blue for water, red for fire, and white for air. "Although most fae can affect elements of all kinds, the element toward which a fae is most inclined is that by which he is defined."

I stared at Sherus' flaming red hair, and all became clear to me. "You're a fae of fire, aren't you?"

He nodded.

"Which is why I have the power to manipulate fire?"

"Correct."

One way or another, fire seems to run in my family...

"Please, continue," I urged.

"My father ruled our fiery realm as emperor, but he wasn't as qualified as my grandfather— although even in his time we'd never gotten on well with the water fae." *So Sherus is royalty. Interesting.* My father, lacking tact and intelligence, ended up sparking a feud between our realm and theirs. It spiraled into an all-out war, and we desperately needed assistance in battle if we were to ever overcome them. But my father—as proud as he was foolish— refused to seek the help of others. So I did what any man of my lineage would do. For the sake of our people, I led a rebellion and overturned my father. Once he was beheaded, all eyes were on me—the late king's only son—for a solution." He crossed his arms over his chest, memories whirling in his eyes as he stared at his realm. "My sister and I searched far and wide for allies, but fae are not the most, shall we say, *liked* of creatures. Certainly none of our other elemental brothers would come to our aide. In the end, the only option we had was to accept the help of ghouls... and in the process we formed a pact with them."

"What pact exactly?" It was Nuriya who posed this question, her voice still uneven from the trauma of last night.

"A pact that was overseen by the oracle twins. In exchange for their manpower in battle, we would agree to serve the ghouls by supplying them with ten thousand ghosts within the span of fifty Earth years."

I grimaced. I didn't have to wonder much why fae were so disliked.

"If we failed to meet the quota, we would become servants of the ghouls for a hundred years more. Still, our end of the deal seemed comparatively light, compared to the valuable service the ghouls were providing us," Sherus continued. "But I should've given more thought to it. At the time, I was desperate. All along, the ghouls knew that they were tricking us. They knew such a number would be nigh impossible to achieve." He glanced at me. "Procuring ghosts is harder than one would think."

Oh, how sorry I feel for you.

"Most do pass to the other side, and those who remain

behind are not so easy to catch. So we found ourselves, and still find ourselves, in a mess. I tried to keep the morale up among my council, but even I have accepted that no matter how hard we work, we will never meet the ghouls' demands." He ran a hand over his face. Then he set his eyes back on the jinn. "So this is where you come in… We need you to annul our pact."

I wondered why a witch—or a group of witches—couldn't have helped him with that. It would have saved me a hell of a lot of trouble… but then, I guessed, I ought to have saved the Nasiris from the Drizans regardless. "And you couldn't use witches because…"

"No witch would be strong enough. The oracles, being freaks of nature, have their own brand of magic. One best suited to a jinni's capabilities. Though even jinn can't break the pact."

I frowned. *"What?"*

"The oracles created the pact between us and the ghouls to be unbreakable… even by themselves. Otherwise what meaning would the pact have? It would be worthless, both to us and the ghouls, if it could be broken. However, since the oracles were overseers of the pact, there is another way the jinn could free us from it."

"What?" I asked, weary of where he was going with all this.

"Kill the oracle sisters."

The jinn surrounding me gasped. Then a deathly silence enshrouded us. It felt like Sherus had just walloped my skull with a brick.

Kill Pythia? Kill Hortencia?

I couldn't allow that. I wouldn't.

"They can see the future," I said to Sherus, exasperated. "How could the jinn possibly murder them?" *Assuming we were even willing to try.* "They would have seen them coming already, God knows how many hundreds of years before."

"That's for your jinn to figure out," Sherus said, looking mildly irritated by now. "If I knew how, I wouldn't be placing the task in their hands, would I?"

His eyes swept over my jinn companions once more before he began to drift away from us. "I will give your jinn three days, Benjamin Novak. And I'm sure I don't need to remind you what will happen to you again if they fail..."

Crap.

"Oh, and one more thing to keep in mind," Sherus added. "We fae have a considerable influence over Earth's elements—the power to effect natural disasters... Let's just say I would suggest your jinn don't fail in this, if you have any affection for your home realm at all."

With that, he dashed away.

BEN

Natural disasters. What did the bastard mean by that? Was he threatening to cause catastrophes on Earth? Had he been blackmailing me? Or perhaps adding an extra incentive, as if keeping my body wasn't already incentive enough?

I hadn't thought it was possible for a man to be put under more stress than I was now. *You're going to get your life stripped from you, lose everyone you love and be kidnapped back to Nightmare Land, and then let's lump in jeopardizing the entire human planet while we're at it...*

There was no curse word strong enough to use in that moment.

Drawing in a deep breath, I turned to face the others.

Everyone looked at me, clueless.

But I knew what I had to do. There was only one thing I could do. I had to try to make contact with Hortencia again—*augh*—and beg for some scraps to help me figure out this mess.

I thought back to the last time I'd visited her cave. Had that only been yesterday? She hadn't even been there— something that had come as a surprise to even Aisha. And when she'd revealed herself via that potion, she'd looked so... old.

I wonder...

Could that have anything to do with this? The fae's intention to kill her and her sister? Had that been why she'd uprooted so unexpectedly?

Placing my hand on the small of River's back and drawing her to me, I addressed everyone. "We need to head to Hortencia's cave." *And hope she has another little bottle waiting for me there, containing some clue as to what the hell I'm supposed to do now.*

***

Aisha and the other jinn knew where Hortencia's cave was located—although none of them seemed to know much at all about her twin, Pythia.

Once we had arrived outside the cave, I decided that it

was best for only three of us to enter, the same three as before: River, Aisha and me.

Trudging through the tunnel, we reached her front door. I didn't bother knocking this time; the door wasn't locked, anyway. When we strode inside, the small room was exactly how we'd left it. Certainly there were no signs of the oracle having returned. The empty bottle that I'd drunk from still sat on the table, along with the note she'd left.

I gazed around, desperately hoping there would be another bottle here. Another note. Another *something*.

"Oh, look!" River pointed upward and my eyes shot to the rocky ceiling.

Somebody had scrawled a note with white chalk, so bold and jagged it looked creepy.

"Everyone has something to hide."

I stared at it, unblinking.

She already told me this last time I had a meeting with her. What does she mean by it now?

"What if she means... herself?" River suggested.

"What would Hortencia have to hide?" I muttered.

River shrugged, then cast her eyes around the room again. "Maybe... Maybe it's an invitation to dig a little deeper. I dunno..."

"Maybe she's hiding something in here?" Aisha said, catching on to River's train of thought.

"Let's search deeper then," I said, and the three of us began searching the room—something that didn't take long, since there wasn't much to search. When I reached the oven, to my surprise I found a book inside. A thick, dusty, fabric-bound book.

"Look at this," I murmured, capturing the girls' attention as I placed the tome on top of the table. A cloud of dust rose in the air as I opened it and turned to the first page, making River cough.

What is this? It must have been old, for the paper was yellowed, and the small black writing—Hortencia's handwriting—was faded. Not too faded to read, however...

As I began to scan the page, River and Aisha stood on either side, reading along with me. I'd gotten halfway down the first page when I realized that this was some kind of journal that the oracle had been keeping. Much of what I read didn't even make sense to me, and seemed more like ramblings without a thread of thought behind them. It felt creepy to be reading this, like a window into her mad mind. A dozen more pages in however, the sentences began to make more sense, until I realized that what I was reading were confessions. Retellings of some truly atrocious acts carried out by her and her sister.

Deliberately misleading a young werewolf family into being caught by a group of black witches. Destroying relationships by planting doubts in each person's mind. Even sparking wars between opposing clans. All of this for no reason other than spite. The way she wrote was sickening. I could practically feel her glee emanating from the pages.

"How did she write all this without eyes?" River wondered softly next to me.

"No idea," I murmured, my mind still drenched in her confessions.

I continued reading until the writing came to an abrupt stop, only one third of the way through the book. She hadn't even finished the sentence she'd started. It just trailed off. The rest of the book was empty except for the very last page where another note was written—one that I could only assume was meant for me:

"Don't you think we deserve to die?"

BEN

Deserve to die?

What is she trying to communicate to me?

"Truthfully," Aisha muttered, drawing in a breath, "I never knew those two sisters were so meddling."

Meddling, was putting it politely.

River slid onto my lap and flipped back through the pages again. She stopped at the section where the writing ended. "Why does it stop here?" She furrowed her brows, leaning closer to the pages.

"Maybe she just got bored of journaling." Aisha shrugged.

I wasn't sure about this. I couldn't be sure of anything with these oracles. But after all my prior dealings with her, I couldn't help but try to read into every single detail, and wonder if it could be some kind of cryptic message to lead me forward.

I turned back to the last page again, to the question she had proposed to me. *Do they deserve to die?*

By most people's measures, I would say yes, certainly. Though I was not God. It was not for me to mete out justice for incidents I had no involvement in. Especially when they had not done anything to harm me directly... well, sort of.

Even after paging through Hortencia's confessions, I still didn't think I had it in me to murder them in cold blood— even if such a thing were possible.

I lingered at the back page a moment longer, then, heaving a sigh, I carried it back to the oven, intending to replace it while I thought about what we could do next. But as I opened the oven this time, I realized that there was something else in here, something that I had not seen before due to my surprise over the book. I had missed a letter, laid out on the tray. It must have been tucked right beneath the book. Replacing the book, I drew out the letter and flattened it against the table, so the three of us could read it together.

"No matter what justifications might be going through your righteous little mind, I and my sister do, indeed, deserve to die. Hence, what follows are instructions on how to find us both... and, in the process, complete your training."

Training? *Huh?*

"This letter will manifest one directive at a time, and you must complete them all, exactly as described. Stray from the orders even once, and you will receive no more instructions. You will never find me or my sister. Follow blindly, pretty boy, and you shall find that which you seek."

"Pretty boy?" River couldn't help but smirk.

My mind, however, was fixed on another part of her note entirely. *"... You shall find that which you seek."*

But what do I seek?

For God's sake, I don't want to murder anyone. I just want to live a normal, physical life with River!

The note on the paper faded and was replaced with a smaller line of text:

"Task one: Return to your body in Cruor and burn it. You may take your half-blood with you, and also your jinni—for the purpose of speed. Remember, you only have three days."

Like I need a reminder.

"Three days to kill them," Aisha said, more to herself than anyone else. "It looks like she wants to take you on a treasure hunt to find her and..."

"Kill her?" River asked, brows raised. "Really? Why would she invite Ben to kill her?"

None of us had any rational answers. I lowered my eyes to the parchment again, focusing on the first task still written there, stubborn, unmoving. *Unmoving until we complete the task.*

Cruor. That sure was one place in the universe I'd hoped to never return to. And we'd have to find my body. Would it even still be there after all this time? The oracle obviously thought so.

I stood up, folding the letter and tucking it into River's back pocket, since I had no pockets of my own. "Keep this safe in there," I told her.

"We're seriously going to Cruor?"

"What else do we do?" I said. "We don't need to think about killing them yet. We may not even get that far and maybe, just maybe, she's got something else up her sleeve that she is not revealing yet... We've no choice but to do what she says."

River swallowed hard, while Aisha shrugged, like it wasn't such a big deal.

"So," the jinni said, grabbing my and River's hands and pulling us out of the cave. "Let's go..."

***

I explained briefly to the others as we emerged from the cave what had to be done, and although they were horrified, as we had already concluded, there was no other way forward. I wanted to leave River behind, but since Hortencia had specified she should come too, I had no grounds upon which to argue with my fiancée. In the meantime, the jinn and our troop from The Shade insisted they'd wait here for us.

As harrowing as the thought of returning to Cruor was, the journey was relatively simple thanks to Aisha. We soon found ourselves standing on the cold shores of the dark realm of the Elders. My stomach was in knots as I looked around us. The place looked deader than I'd ever seen it. Everything was still—the mountains, even the red-tinged clouds. Almost no breeze. Memories rolled over me: the day Julie had betrayed me, coming face to face with the Elder who had imprinted on me.

"So… if you could tell us where your body is right about now, that would be good," Aisha grumbled, holding a shawl closer around her shoulders.

If Aisha was cold, River must be freezing. I rubbed my hands down her arms as I tried to rack my brain as to the location. I had spent a long time here after leaving my body, being afraid and mulling over what to do next. I'd wandered up and down this same shoreline many times before in my attempt to detach myself.

"Uh, let's head in that direction," I told Aisha, pointing north.

I flew with River, while Aisha floated alongside us. Finally, I spotted the peak—I recognised it even from a distance due to the massive crater that was drilled though it. The crater the Elder had emerged from in his attempt to possess me.

To my shock, my body still lay there, exactly where I'd left it. As I descended, shivers ran through me. I'd forgotten how bizarre the feeling was, to be staring down at oneself... or at least one's body. It was rigid, but didn't show signs of deterioration.

"My God, this is so creepy," River breathed. She gripped my arm hard, as if reassuring herself that I was still standing next to her.

We circled around the body and then I bent down. I placed my fingers against the corpse's forehead. Stone cold. Not much different than when it had been alive.

"Well," I said, realizing how parched my throat had gotten, "now we've got to burn it."

I looked expectantly at Aisha. I might be able to conduct and spread fire, but I wasn't able to create it—at least, it didn't seem so. She bent down, and a blaze billowed from her fingertips. It was so unexpectedly large, it almost touched my and River's ankles. Not wanting to turn into Burning Man again, I staggered back with River, watching as the fire engulfed my previous body. I had expected the jinni to be a little more... subtle about it. I don't know, something a little more ceremonious. It was my funeral, after all. But this was

Aisha, I reminded myself.

My eyes glazed over as I watched the fire consume my body. I experienced an odd twinge in my chest. A pain, almost. It was like something was being ripped from me, and it left me feeling unsteady. Uncertain of my very existence. That what I'd forever identified with was so... material. So destructible.

The bonfire rose higher and higher, choking the air with smoke and stinging our eyes, until all that remained was ashes. This vision I knew would haunt me for the rest of my life.

That's it. My body's gone.

After the fire had died down, we moved to another mountain peak further away just in case the blaze had drawn any attention. The last thing we needed was to encounter an Elder, although admittedly they should still be too weak to cause harm even to River.

Reaching into River's back pocket, I slid out the note and unfolded it. When I spread it out, the note changed before my very eyes. I was surprised by what I read. I'd been expecting to see the next instruction she had for us, but instead, it simply said:

"So long as you burn to live, you shall, with or without breath."

BEN

The message lingered on the page a while, as if she'd wanted me to read it many times, absorb it fully. And as the smoke cleared, revealing the ashes, I did.

I could only assume that this was part of her "training", whatever she had meant by that.

Finally, the note changed:

"Now, as an extension of this first task, follow my directions, for they will lead you to where you need to be."

An extension to this first task? What? She never said a single task might have several layers.

"Ugh," River muttered.

The note changed again:

"Travel to the bottom of this mountain."

We did as instructed.

"Turn right."

We turned right.

"Turn left."

We did.

On and on the instructions went until, finally, she told us to stop outside the entrance to a tunnel.

"Enter."

Tentatively, we entered the mouth of the tunnel and proceeded along its dank, winding depths.

"Stop."

We stopped in our tracks, about halfway through.

"Look at the wall on your left."

Huh? As I examined the grimy wall, at first I saw nothing but...wall. But as I examined it more closely I noticed a slight ridge, which led me to discover that it was actually a hidden door.

"Open it."

We did, and it led us through to another tunnel, the ground and ceiling filled with stalagmites and stalactites. The note kept leading us onward through the gloom, through another door, until we reached a stone staircase leading downward.

Where is this woman taking us?

At the bottom of the staircase was another entrance, only this was locked with a bolt. I instinctively moved to open it, as I'd done the previous two, but then River grasped my arm and held me back. She pointed at the note:

"Don't open it yet, impatient child!"

Annoyed, I waited for the note to change.

"Ask Aisha for a sword."

Aisha handed me one of her blades.

"Now, enter with Aisha and slay all that you see."

"What?" River and I gasped at once.

Slay what inside? I look at the door with alarm.

"Are we really doing this?" River whispered, looking more nervous than I'd seen her.

"You stay here," I told her.

Clutching my sword, with Aisha close behind me, I slowly unbolted the stone entrance and ground it open to reveal… a dark chamber. Maybe even a dungeon. An apparently empty one. Pools of liquid scattered the ground, and a revolting smell hit me. Like… corpse juice mixed with mold. Yet there were no bodies on the floor.

Aisha and I dared move further inside.

"There's nothing to slay here," I whispered. "It's just an empty cave."

"Oh no, it's not!" Aisha gasped suddenly. She pointed up at the ceiling.

The jagged ceiling was lined with… bodies? Bare, stark-white bodies, clinging to the ceiling. They were utterly emaciated, their skin disgustingly thin.

Holy…

Aisha finished my thought for me.

"What the hell are they?" I hissed.

"I know what these are," she breathed. "They are Bloodless!"

"Bloodless?"

Before she could explain, the bodies began to peel off the ceiling and drop down to the floor. There were so many of them, I could barely even keep them all in my sight as they began lunging toward us.

A yelp came from behind me. River.

One of the "Bloodless" had circled Aisha and me and darted for the open door.

"Don't let it touch River!" Aisha screamed. "And don't let it bite you either!"

Bite?

I hurtled toward the creature moving for River and managed to reach the door in time to shut it before it could reach her. Now we were in darkness. The aura of my body gave off some light, and Aisha quickly made a fire blaze in one corner of the room to help us see better. Several Bloodless lunged for me at once. *What the hell are these things?* They had fangs and claws, characteristics of vampires, and yet they were unlike any vampire I'd ever seen.

"You need to hack them to bits!" Aisha bellowed from across the room, as she began to do just that.

I lifted myself into the air and rained blows down on the creatures beneath me, even as they began springing up to reach me. I managed to sever several of their heads, and then, following Aisha's example, descended to hack the rest of their bodies to bits. The name Aisha had given them was appropriate. As much as I chopped and slashed, there was not a single speck of blood on my sword.

Aisha and I continued dodging and slicing as they attempted to bite us, and eventually, we managed to fell them all. It was hard to count now that they were all mangled up, but there appeared to be over two dozen.

We backed out of the room and returned to River. She flung herself at me the second I stepped through the door.

"What were those things?" she breathed, holding me in a trembling embrace.

"Bloodless," Aisha wheezed, still catching her breath. I wondered why she hadn't just used her magic, as she seemed to have recovered much of it since we'd retrieved some of her family. Maybe she enjoyed the fight. "They're a kind of vampire," she explained.

Then the jinni began to recount what had happened to

her before her arrival in The Shade. By the time she was finished, my jaw was on the floor. Bloodless. A kind of mutation of vampires, who'd been deprived of blood. Who could turn humans, and even other vampires into one of them? Could they turn other species? And why did the oracle ask us to kill them? And Julie had become one of them. According to Aisha, she had been turned by one on the small island that connected the ogres' realm to Earth. And then the two of them had ventured away from it... to where exactly? Disconcertingly, Aisha didn't know. "They could be anywhere," she said with a shrug.

My head swam with questions as we whizzed back up the staircase and along the tunnels.

When we arrived outside again, the note changed:

"There exists evil in the world that should never be given a second chance."

***

The three of us were still mulling over her words as a new instruction appeared on the faded parchment:

"Your second task awaits you in Dagger Mountain. Flutter there now, fairy."

"I wish she would stop calling me that," I muttered.

River snorted. "At least we're officially on the 'second task' now," she said.

"So." I heaved a sigh. "Dagger Mountain. Where is that exactly?" I asked Aisha.

I felt worried when Aisha tensed. "Uh, yeah… that's back in The Dunes."

"What?" River and I exclaimed at once.

"But it's well away from any jinn settlement," Aisha added quickly. "I'm just trying to recall where exactly it is. Definitely far away from the Drizans' palace. I've visited there perhaps twice in my entire life, but I should be able to remember how to get back… hopefully."

"You'd better," I said.

Aisha ended up getting us lost. We drifted aimlessly around the menacing land of The Dunes looking for the mountain. We found a mountain range—several actually—but none looked right to Aisha, and as night fell, we still hadn't found it.

"Let's… let's wait till morning," Aisha said, as we moved deeper into the night. She looked nervous while we gazed down upon the eerily quiet landscape.

"That's like, hours wasted," I seethed.

"Yes, but I-I don't feel comfortable roaming around now," Aisha said. "I mean it. There are… strange things that lurk in The Dunes after dark."

"What strange things?" River whispered, her face paling.

What strange things? I almost laughed. *How about giant*

jinni-scorpion mutants?

"Neither of you need to know," Aisha snapped, quite flustered all of a sudden. *What could be worse than what I've already seen?* "Because we won't meet any of them, if we do as I say and stop for the night."

It so disturbed me to see Aisha nervous like this that I didn't question her any more. "Okay," I said. "Where should we rest?"

"We'll find a cave, somewhere in these mountains," she said.

"Uh, yeah. You'll need to smoke out any scorpions before I take River into one of those."

"Obviously," Aisha breathed, still irritable.

We drifted around for the next half hour scouting for a suitable cave. Once Aisha had chosen one, she told us to wait outside while she drifted in. She literally did smoke the place out. Smoke billowed out from the entrance, bringing with it a toxic smell. Coughing, River and I moved farther back, waiting for Aisha to emerge.

"All right," she said, dusting off her hands as she walked out. "There were definitely no giant scorpions in there and…" She pointed to a dozen rats, spiders and other creepy-crawlies scampering out of the cave and into cracks in the walls. "There shouldn't be anything else left either."

"That stuff smells strong enough to poison us, too," River

said, still coughing.

Aisha rolled her eyes as I landed with River on the ridge outside the cave. Then she sparked up a fire in the center.

"The Dunes' nights are harsh," she said, stoking the flames and raising them higher. "Almost as harsh as the days' heat."

I had to be sure to keep my distance from the bonfire. I moved to a wall and sat down. River flopped down next to me. Aisha sat with her back facing us.

River nuzzled her head against me. I kissed the top of it. "Do you want to get some sleep?"

She leaned closer against me. "I'll try."

"Then let's lie flat." I lay down on my side across the dry ground and gathered River to me as she did the same. Her skin was cold as always. I kissed her lips, tasting them one at a time. She reached for my hand and flattened our palms against each other.

"You still don't have a ring," I remembered.

River smiled and planted kisses over my knuckles. "I will soon." Her turquoise eyes were filled with such conviction. I wished I could believe her without doubt.

As the night progressed, we kissed some more and cuddled, but didn't talk much. There was not much more that we could say that we weren't already saying with our eyes. We both shared the same desperate hope, the same blind faith that however crazy this path was that Hortencia was leading us on, it had to work out. I couldn't bring myself to think about what would happen if it didn't. I'd spiral into a depression I'd never escape from. *It just has to work out.*

Once River's eyes began to droop and she eventually fell asleep, I scooped her up from the ground—realizing it was too cold for her here—and moved a little closer to the fire. I positioned her on my lap and cradled her, one arm beneath her legs and the other around her waist, while her head rested against my chest. I gazed down at her beautiful, peaceful face. Unable to keep my lips off her, I trailed them softly down the bridge of her nose.

Aisha still sat in the same spot, back turned. Was she keeping watch? Or did she just want her own space?

"Hey," I called to her in a whisper. She twisted to face me, raising a brow. "Come sit with us."

Heaving a sigh, she ambled over and sank down next to me against the wall. Her eyes returned to the shadowy desert stretched out all around us.

"Are you okay?" I asked her.

"Yeah."

"Still feeling nervous?"

She slanted me a glance. "Yes," she replied, as though it was a stupid question. "But up here... we should be okay. I just need to keep watch."

"Keep watch for what?"

She shivered. "They say it's bad luck to talk about monsters at night-time. They say it attracts them."

"They? Them?"

"Just stop asking, Benjamin," Aisha snapped, loud enough to cause River to stir.

I hushed the jinni.

"Don't ask again," she said in a low tone.

I joined Aisha in staring out at the dunes. A span of silence fell between us, the only sounds being the crackling fire and the distant chirping of some kind of nocturnal animal.

"At least I have half my family back," Aisha said, changing the subject. She drew a shuddering breath. "I really thought I'd lost them all."

"I'm... truly sorry for the loss of your men."

She nodded, swallowing hard. "Well, I should thank you for helping us... me." She chewed on her lower lip, her eyes flickering from me to River. Then she looked down at her hands, which were clenched. "I missed you, you know," she said in a whisper, meeting my eyes again. The look of longing in her eyes took me aback. She'd never hidden the fact that she had a crush on me, but I'd never really thought it was much more than that.

"I, uh, should tell you that I proposed to River," I said, not wanting her to think she had any leeway with me.

A flash of bitterness curled her lips.

"Oh," she said.

Another silence.

"You know," I said, clearing my throat, "I noticed Horatio seems to—"

"Yes, I know," Aisha said.

"Know what?" I prodded.

"That he likes me."

"Don't you like him?"

She looked away, and a blush crept to her cheeks. She bit down hard on her lower lip. "I, um... I suppose I do," she said.

The shade of her cheeks betrayed just what an understatement that was.

Then she swiveled, looking restless all of a sudden. She exhaled sharply, and her mouth twitched, as if to say something but holding herself back.

"What?" I asked.

"I-I just wonder. Did you ever like me, like, at all? Or have you always hated me?"

I sighed. "I have never hated you, Aisha. And I certainly don't hate you now. I'm not going to deny you were annoying as hell when we first met... but now you're my friend. A friend who, quite honestly, I wouldn't be able to do without right now."

Dimples formed in her cheeks as she smiled. Her eyes glistened in the firelight, and for a moment I thought she was about to get all teary.

"Okay," she said, swallowing. "I guess that's good enough."

There was another pause before I broached the subject of Horatio again. "If you like that prince, you should tell him, you know." I cast her a teasing glance. "Don't forget, now that your sisters and cousins are free, he's got a lot of girls to choose from…"

Aisha shoved me in the shoulder. "What are you now, a matchmaker as well as a fairy?"

I cracked a tired smile as I stroked River's forehead. "Not exactly. Just… a firm believer in never taking anything for granted in this life."

***

Aisha and I sat together, chatting quietly and trying to keep our thoughts on brighter things than the obstacles ahead of us. She told me more about her childhood and her history with Horatio, which soon transformed into a monologue of endless circular arguments about why she might, or might not, end up dating him.

"I mean, I like him but… do I *really* like him?" She posed the question with a profound expression, as though she were pondering the meaning of life.

"Uh… I'm pretty sure that you do."

"What would you know?" She shoved me in the shoulder again, after which I shut up and let her sink back into her logic-forsaken rambling. *Heaven forbid I suggest something, like, conclusive…*

I was glad when River woke up an hour or so later. The conversation became a bit more stimulating.

We'd just started speculating again about the oracle's true intention for this bizarre quest she was leading me on when Aisha abruptly raised a hand and shushed us with such urgency, spit flew from her mouth.

Her eyes were frozen on a spot in the desert and the next thing I knew, she'd extinguished the fire, plunging us all into darkness.

"What?" I breathed.

"There," Aisha mouthed, pointing.

I strained to see through the night. Finally I spotted it. A hulking stick-like figure in the distance, standing motionless in the sand. It was only a silhouette in the moonlight, but I could make out two long legs which seemed to curve into feet, and long, thin arms that extended to flat… webbed hands? Its head was perhaps the creepiest thing about it. It was thrice the size it should have been in comparison to the rest of its body, and it was almost perfectly circular. *What has a head that round and that big?* Something told me it wasn't a creature I'd recognize from Earth.

It moved suddenly—shockingly fast—and in a very unsettling way. It hopped almost like a kangaroo, only adding to its eerie appearance.

"What is that?" I demanded beneath my breath.

"It's a hunkri," Aisha whispered.

"A what?" I hissed.

"A hunkri. Just… shh. Be quiet and it should pass."

It didn't look like it was passing. It looked like it was heading straight for our mountain.

"Shouldn't we move from—?" I whispered.

"Yes," Aisha breathed, realizing her wishful thinking was just that. "Let's leave."

"Oh!" River let out a gasp. "There's another one!"

She was pointing to our right, where, shockingly close, another one of the creatures slunk against the mountain wall, climbing rapidly toward us. This one I could see more clearly beneath the light of the moon. *What the…* Its thin, sticklike body was covered in mud-brown scales, and its huge head… most of that was a frilled, pleated skin flap surrounding its bulging-eyed, lizard-like face.

"I thought you said we'd be safe in a cave," I hissed through gritted teeth.

"I didn't expect us to come across freaking hunkris!" Aisha

shot back. "I didn't even think they lived in these p—"

"Let's get out of here!" I bundled River onto my back and we launched into the sky.

A piercing scream emanated from the creatures' throats in unison, matching eerily in pitch. Then, to my horror, wings I hadn't even noticed unfolded behind their back. Wings like a bat's. Without warning, they bolted into the sky after us.

"Vanish us!" I yelled to Aisha, hurrying closer to her.

"Okay!" she screamed.

Aisha vanished... but River and I didn't.

In the split second before she'd used her vanishing powers, something long, hot and intensely sticky had wound around my leg, holding me back. When I gazed down, it was to see a colossal white-as-snow tongue extending from the mouth of one of the hunkris beneath us. It wrapped like a snake around my leg. I couldn't even thin myself, or I would drop River. And Aisha had vanished.

River swore as the hunkri jerked us downward with its tongue.

A blade. I need a blade. I fumbled for a belt, but remembered I had none. Everything we'd traveled with, we'd left on the cliff's edge.

"Ben!"

Oh, thank God. Aisha reappeared. She shrieked as she saw the tongue around my ankle.

"Take River!" I shouted, even as the hunkri closed the distance between us.

"No, Ben, I can try—"

"There's no time!" I roared. "Take her!"

I practically flung River at Aisha in my panic. The jinni thankfully caught her in the air. Then, overpowered by the hunkri's strength, I was pulled right down into its rapidly expanding toothless jaws, mouth and neck. Almost like an anaconda, the creature expanded to accommodate my size and the next thing I knew, I'd been sucked right inside, down its slimy throat, and found myself in the chamber of its gut.

Oh. My. God.

Can this night get any worse?

BEN

I tried to thin myself, but horrifyingly, I couldn't pass through the walls of its gut. I didn't know why. Was it because I was covered with too much of the creature's gut grime? Or was there something special about its constitution that prevented me from passing through it?

Whatever the case, I was certain I was going to puke inside this hunkri. Murky-looking stomach juices sloshed around as the hunkri hurtled through the sky. A disgusting gaseous smell overwhelmed me. I had to try to escape through its mouth, but gazing up, I couldn't see an exit. It was like the roof of its mouth had sealed over me, locking me inside.

I pounded with my fists against the side of the creature,

hoping to make it feel as sick as I was feeling. It didn't seem to hamper its flight at all. If anything, it felt like it was speeding faster.

Where is Aisha?

I'd been hoping she could hurl a curse at the creature after catching River. No luck there. I prayed the girls were all right and hadn't been claimed by the other monster.

Without warning, the hunkri's stomach contracted. I was tipped upside down on my head. Its mouth opened and then I was falling, through its neck, jaws, until my body hit a sharp, rocky surface.

Before I could even orientate myself enough to attempt escape, the hunkri's wide, powerful webbed feet kicked me right in the gut, sending me rolling until I slipped over... a ledge.

The next thing I was aware of was heat. Heat unlike anything I'd experienced before. I had plunged into a thick, gritty liquid of some sort. I couldn't breathe. I waded through it, fighting to reach the surface. As I opened my eyes...

Oh, wow. No wonder I feel hot.

Bright red lava bubbled around me. Charred black walls surrounded me on all sides. The hunkri had kicked me into a crater filled with molten lava. Directly above was an opening—where the lava no doubt would spurt—and beyond that was the dark sky.

This is… something.

My whole body was blazing with fire. But unlike the burning sensation I'd experienced earlier, back in the Drizans' palace, this was unpleasant. Intensely unpleasant. Like someone was stabbing me with daggers all over my body. And it was getting more unpleasant by the minute. I might be a fire fae—whatever that meant—but was there only so much of an element that a fae could take?

A bubble of lava nearby exploded in my face. Then came a deep splash. As if I wasn't in enough hot water already, the hunkri had just dived into the pool and resurfaced next to me. Grabbing hold of my head, it submerged me again in the lava.

Ugh, get off me, you bastard. What was it trying to do? *I'm not interested in bath time with you.*

I managed to resurface, but the creature only grabbed me and pushed me down again. I could imagine how comical this would look to any onlooker, this lively game of whack-a-mole, but humor was the last thing on my brain as I fell short of breath. I managed to distance myself enough to resurface and gasp in more than three seconds of air before it hammered me down again. It was like it wanted to cook me or something. Since it didn't have teeth… was it trying to cook me into a homogenous mush and then eat me?

Instead of continuing the foolery of attempting to distance myself from it, I decided to move right up to it. How I wished that I possessed the claws of a vampire in that moment. Gripping hold of the webbed hand that descended to bash me down again, I dug my fingers into it, holding it in place, before kicking sharply upward at its thin elbow joint. Bone cracked, followed by an obnoxious scream.

It flailed and let go of me, allowing me to rise to the surface.

"Ben!" River's voice echoed down from above.

I gaped upward to see her hovering with Aisha high above the opening of the crater. At least they were okay. They'd found the hunkri's trail. My head pounding with a migraine like no other, I shot upward. But not for long. Even with a broken arm, the hunkri wasn't letting go of its meal so easily. It lunged for me again with its tongue, this time gripping me by the waist.

My vision was becoming blurry. It felt like my brain was overheating. I had to... get out of... this heat. Whatever strength I had remaining ebbed out of me as the hunkri dragged me back down. I was slowing down. Shutting down.

"Ben!" River screamed. "Do something, Aisha!"

River.

No. I can't go back into the bath. Not back beneath the surface.

With a guttural roar I hoped would rouse the rest of me, just as the hunkri had drawn me a few feet above the lava, I grabbed hold of its frilled skin flap behind its ears. Planting both feet against the side of its head, I leveraged the stance to pull hard, tearing the frill from its head in one place.

Again it flailed, and this time appeared to be in more pain. A surprising amount of pain for a small tear.

I shot up and as I flew away, looked more closely at my captor. I realized that it hadn't been the rip that had caused it to release me, but a leaden spear sticking out of its chest… That would explain it.

Aisha drifted down toward me on her own, licking her lower lip in satisfaction as she eyed the hunkri.

"Thanks for that," I rasped. "Though I could have used that help a bit sooner. Where's River?"

She led me out of the crater and pointed toward a cluster of rocks where River was standing, arms wrapped tensely around her waist.

I wanted to pick her up, but reminded myself I would need to wait a while before touching River again, unless I wanted a fried fiancée.

Aisha picked up River and together we soared to find a safer place to recover. We found another ledge nearby. After the jinni doused me with showers of water and ice, my head became clearer, the pain in my skin and brain ebbing away.

"Talk about hot," River said, once she was finally able to touch me again. She stretched her palm over my forehead.

"Won't find hotter than me, baby..." I muttered. *Ouch.* My throat still felt so parched. Leaning back against the wall, I breathed in deeply, rubbing my temples. Then in a panic I asked, "Do you still have the letter?" I feared that it could've slipped from her pocket during the struggle.

River's hand shot down into her pocket and, to my relief, she pulled it out. I took it from her and unfolded it, to make sure it hadn't been damaged, and in doing so realised that the message had changed already... even though we hadn't completed the second task yet.

"Don't ever get cocky, sugar dust."

Cocky. It took a few moments just to get over my own anger at being called cocky after what she'd just put me through. I bet she'd foreseen all this: Aisha getting lost, the hunkris happening to pass our way on just that very night. Of course she would've.

But, reading the note again after I'd calmed my temper, I guessed what she was trying to say was that even now I had procured this fae body, I could never take it for granted. I also supposed that, truth be told, I had sunk into thinking that securing this fae body would be the be-all and end-all. This was her not-so-subtle reminder that I was in no way invincible.

Well, she'd accomplished what she'd wanted to achieve. I couldn't deny that. This little hunkri incident would stay plastered to my brain for a long, long time.

RIVER

I was still recovering from the shock alongside Ben. All I wanted was to get out of this horrible, frightening place as soon as possible, get done with whatever the damn oracle wanted us to do, and return to The Shade. I prayed that we were nearing the last of her nasty surprises.

Morning arrived; at least now we had the sun. We decided that Ben should rest a little more before continuing our search for Dagger Mountain, but Aisha said that we should move from these mountains—something I could not agree more with. Even though Aisha said night-time was the most dangerous time to be outside in The Dunes, I did not want to run any risks. She took us to an oasis instead. A real oasis, much larger than I had expected it to be. It was like a mini jungle in the midst of the desert: luscious trees, bushes and flowers, and even a reservoir of water.

Ben's skin was still rough from the trauma, grit from the lava still clinging to him in places. I imagined this cool water would have been soothing as he slid inside.

"While you're resting here," Aisha said, "I think I should get a headstart in looking for the mountain. I'll be back soon."

"Wait," Ben said. "Will we be safe here without you?"

"You'll be okay. As I said, I won't be long."

With that, she flew away. Ben shrugged at me. "We'll have to hope she's right."

I perched myself on the edge of the lake, refreshing my feet in the water. I watched as Ben began to swim up and down, his powerful body quickly crossing the reservoir.

Then he swam back to me.

"Aren't you coming in?"

I hadn't been planning to go fully in, but finding myself with this unexpected private time with Ben, there was nothing more I wanted in that moment.

Stripping to my underwear, I folded my top and pants and placed them securely on the branch of a tree before approaching the water. I slipped into the water, my bare stomach brushing against Ben's abdomen as he pulled me to him. I rested my arms over his shoulders, my fingers grazing the water's surface as he kissed me.

"We should get this grit off you," I murmured.

Leaving him, I swam to the bank and looked around for anything that I could use as a scrubber. I was leery of plucking any plants or leaves though, in case they were poisonous.

"Guess I'll have to use my nails," I said, swimming back to him and grinning.

"Good thing you don't have claws, then," he said.

He extended his right arm to me where he had a cluster of the black, gritty substance. I began to gently scratch away at it, trying not to scratch his actual skin. The stuff was stuck fast, but slowly it began to crumble, revealing smooth skin beneath—or at least, as smooth as a man could feel.

"Thank you," Ben said, smiling as I announced that I'd finished. He gathered me to him. "And how much do I owe you for that?"

"Hm, you could just... not get yourself killed again? Would that be too much to ask?"

"That depends on the oracle's next task."

Ugh. What will she ask for next?

Ben's mouth closed around the base of my throat, where he sucked gently at my skin. "But for now, you have me to yourself. And I have you."

He pulled me toward the opposite end of the pool, where there was a small covering of leaves, sheltering a patch of water like a canopy. When we ducked into it, it gave a beautiful sense of privacy.

Settling into one corner, we went still, gazing into each other's eyes. Now we were alone, and his body felt so tense against mine.

I bit my lower lip, my desire for him making me tingle all over. I moved for his right ear, catching his lobe between my lips before breathing, "I want you."

His right hand sank into my hair and he pulled my head back so he could meet my eyes again. His expression had gone quite serious, his green eyes hooded and intense. I shivered as he claimed my lips passionately, his fingers moving up my back to the clasp of my bra. He caught the bra's catch, and I was breathless as he slowly let it fall. Then his hands slid to my waist and he eased off my underpants. Fire leapt in his eyes as he took me in, every part of me, unhurriedly, as though time held no value. I reached for his undergarments and gently loosened and pushed them away. My heart pounded as he was suddenly just as bare as me, the only thing between us a small passage of water. A passage he closed quickly.

My abdomen quivered as it pressed against his. Our bodies molded together, his hands and lips continuing to caress and explore. It felt like the blood in my veins had been replaced with molten lava.

"You're a goddess, River," he whispered, drawing a breath.

I threaded my fingers through his hair before wrapping my legs around his hips. I closed my eyes. "Ben," I breathed. *I wish you would just... that we could just...*

"Guys!"

Aisha's voice blasted through the canopy like a foghorn, shattering our illusion of privacy into a thousand pieces. Ben and I froze, our chests heaving, staring at each other, our wide eyes filled with the same expression: disappointment. Agonizing disappointment. *She had to return just now?* We'd been looking for that mountain for almost half a day so far, and just when... *Has she found it already?*

It killed me to detach myself from him. We were forced to scramble around in the water looking for our underwear. Luckily the water was clear, and we spotted them at the bottom. Ben retrieved them and we quickly put them on before swimming back out into view.

Aisha was hovering overhead, eyes darting around for us.

"Oh, there you are," she yelled down, her face glistening with sweat, beaming and triumphant. "I found it!"

"Uh, that's great," Ben said. I didn't think he could sound more unenthusiastic if he tried. His lips and cheeks were still flushed, as I was sure mine were.

"Well, get your clothes on already," Aisha scolded with a roll of her eyes. "Let's go!"

BEN

Aisha. She was both a gift and a curse. At any other moment, I would have been thrilled that she had found the mountain so soon. *But it just had to be at that moment.*

Once River and I were dressed, Aisha transported us away from the oasis and when we reappeared again, we were standing at the foot of a giant blackish mountain, whose single peak was as sharp as a dagger. A haze of thick mist rotated around the top of it.

"Dagger Mountain," Aisha said, with a flourish of her hand. "I knew it wasn't far from that oasis."

"Okay." I heaved a sigh of relief. "So we've completed Hortencia's second objective to reach the mountain. Let's check the note."

River removed it from her back pocket and unfolded it. A new message was already waiting for us there.

"Climb to the top, take your lover with you, and be sure to remain in your physical form. Remember, failing to obey my instructions precisely will result in me disappearing and never assisting you again."

Assisting. But is that really what you're doing here?

My gaze panned to the top of the mountain.

"That's really... really high," River said nervously, as she craned her neck to look too.

"In case you haven't guessed from the smoke," Aisha added, "this is actually another volcano."

Great.

"Do you have any idea why the oracle would want me to climb up there with River?" I asked the jinni.

She shrugged, shaking her head. "No clue. I don't even know exactly what's at the top; I've never been up there in my life. Never had reason to. I'll keep watch while you're up there, though. Good luck."

Grimacing, I helped River onto my back. Then I drifted upward, my eyes fixed at the top.

"Do you really think this'll be the last thing the oracle will ask us to do?" River's voice was higher pitched than normal.

"No clue." Anything was possible with Hortencia.

Literally, anything.

We fell into silence as I continued to fly upward, until River broke out into a violent coughing fit. I paused in the air, craning my neck to look back at her. "You okay, baby?"

She was coughing too much to even answer my question.

"Hey," I said, tensing. I guided her off my back and into my arms. I held her in front of me, leaning her backside against the rocks as I examined her. Her coughing was only becoming worse. "It's this smoke," I breathed. We'd just broached the borders of the dark cloud.

Casting aside all thoughts of the oracle's precise instructions, I immediately hurtled back down the mountain. The lower we sank, the more River's coughing died down. Finally, she was able to talk normally. "Yeah," she said, clutching her throat. "It must have been the smoke."

Being half human, River was clearly more susceptible than me, who hadn't been bothered by it.

"Right." I clenched my jaw, eyes darting upward to the mountain's peak, and then down to the ground where Aisha was hovering. "I'm returning you to the ground."

Fear filled her eyes. "But, Ben, Hortencia said—"

"I know what Hortencia said." Cutting short a debate, I flew her back down to the ground and planted her on the sand.

"Huh?" Aisha's nose wrinkled in confusion. "What are you doing back down here already?"

"I have to continue by myself," I said, sliding out the letter from River's pocket. "It's far too toxic up there for River."

"But the oracle—" Aisha began.

"And if the oracle kicks up a fuss," I went on, "well... so be it."

BEN

Traveling back up the mountain, I flew fully into the cloud of smog. It became so thick that I could barely see two feet in front of me. I climbed higher and higher through the toxic gas, and it started to make even me feel heady.

Finally, I reached the top. The peak was actually not as sharp as it looked from the ground. Its very tip was a wide plateau and in the center bubbled a crater, spewing forth smoke and sparks of fuming lava. I moved around the crater, trying to scope the place out through all the thick fog, and as I'd almost come full circle, I found myself rooted to the spot. There, standing in a corner just ten feet away, was an old woman. An old woman with fleshy pits instead of eyes.

She wore a long black robe.

"Hortencia," I breathed. "You're... you're here." A part of me wondered if this was some kind of illusion brought about by the fumes.

Lowering her hood, she hobbled close to me. She looked so ancient, even more now that I saw her in the flesh. So feeble that she might crack a bone just by walking.

Her shriveled lips curved in a smile that revealed her yellowed teeth. "Good," she croaked. "You passed my second test."

I gaped at her. "What?" *But I didn't even follow your rules.*

Chuckling, she planted a hand around my right forearm and led me away from the middle of the volcano toward a clearer patch of plateau, where the wind was stronger and the air was slightly clearer.

"Some rules, boy, are meant to be broken. That is where the skill lies, of any true leader; deciding which rules should be broken and which should be kept intact."

I still stared at her, wondering where she was going with all of this.

"Why don't you take another peek at your letter," she suggested patronizingly.

I unfolded it to see that the text had changed.

"Place love before law, and you shall live a fruitful, though not flawless, life."

Okay... I guessed my refusing to bring River up here was approved by the oracle. This sure came as a surprise to me. Hortencia hadn't exactly given me the impression that she was the romantic type, and had always struck me as quite callous when it came to finer sentiments like love or awareness of the feelings of others. I narrowed my eyes on her. *Is this really the same Hortencia?*

"What's happened to you?" I asked.

Her mouth stretched in a small smile. "What must happen to all of us."

"What?"

"Never mind that now," she said. "Consult your letter again."

My eyes shot to the parchment to discover a new note.

"What are you waiting for? We're standing right in front of you. Kill us."

There were lots of things about those few words that sent my head into a tailspin, though the first that surfaced was: We *are standing?* Hortencia was here, but I couldn't see...

No sooner had the thought entered my mind than I caught a glimpse of another frail, old women approaching from the other side of the crater. She was exactly the same height as Hortencia and the structure of her face was identical too. The only striking difference between them was that Pythia was stark naked.

I fixed my eyes firmly on Hortencia's face. Apparently Pythia was the more, *ahem*, eccentric of the two.

Pythia slunk up to us, her face panned up to me as she stood beside her sister. They linked hands.

"Well?" Hortencia quirked a practically nonexistent brow. "What are you waiting for?"

My focus returned to the note. "I-I don't understand what you're saying."

"Does this smoke impair your tender little eyes?"

"I can read," I said, exasperated. "But I can't kill you!" Hollow disappointment swelled in the pit of my stomach. All throughout this journey, since the very beginning, I'd been hoping that she would have some trick up her sleeve to get us all out of this—one that wouldn't involve actual murder. That was crazy.

"Why not?" Hortencia asked, frowning. She manifested a blade in her hand and pushed it into mine. "You have the means... and we are ready for it."

I gaped at them in disbelief. *What is going on?*

"I cannot kill you!" I said, discarding the dagger and throwing my hands in the air. "And why would you even want to die?" *None of this makes any sense.*

"Death comes for all of us eventually," Hortencia said. "As you can see by our bodies revealing their natural age, we are well ripe for leaving this Earth... And besides, don't you think we deserve it? After all I showed you about us?"

"I don't care whether you're willing to die or not," I said. "Or whether you deserve it. I'm not the one to do it. Though I will say," I couldn't help but add, "I don't think you're really that bad. Honestly, you just seem... intensely unhappy."

As I said the words, I realized that was exactly what they were. The root of all their meddling seemed born out of frustration. They were unhappy, miserable souls, with a curse in disguise as a gift. Born without eyes, they'd never once been able to experience the true beauty of the world. Even after everything the oracle had put me through, I couldn't bring myself to feel a sliver of hatred for her. Instead I just... pitied her.

Hortencia smiled broadly. "Now that wasn't too painful, was it?" she asked.

"What?" Man. She was tying my brain up in knots. *Is this all a fourth test?*

Hortencia beamed like the Cheshire Cat. "Just as loving is important, so equally is mercy. Remember this, Benjamin." She clutched my wrists and if she'd had eyes, I was certain that they would be boring into me right now.

"I have lived a thousand lives," she said, her voice dropping to a whisper, "none of them my own. But I have witnessed enough mistakes by others to have learnt the secrets to leading a wondrously happy life… I also know the makings of a hero." She paused, removing one hand from me and planting it on her sister's shoulder. "Now I have done many abhorrent things in my years, as has my sister, but at the dusk of life, whoever we are, we wish to look back on something worthy of pride."

I still don't understand.

"Let me tell you something, child. I've never been proud of anything I've done… until I started helping you." *Huh?* A clammy hand reached up to my face and patted my cheek. "In time you will understand exactly what I mean by this. For now, just know that the world in a couple of decades' time will be in great need of men like you. All final boundaries will collapse, and that which should never be fused will fuse. You will live through this time and it will not be easy. You will be forced to become the hero whom… whom I have been attempting to train you to become. In the brief time that we've spent together, I've tried to give you a crash course, to instill in you a selection of morals I have learnt and that I believe will serve you well in the future."

My head spun. *Crash course is an appropriate term, all right…*

"Why… why would you do this, though? Why would you even care?"

She smiled, bittersweet. "To leave this world with a lighter burden on my shoulders, I suppose. If you become the warrior that I see within you, and set an example for others to follow, fate might smile a little more kindly on me… for where I go next."

"But… Hortencia. You just said that this was a test, and I should not kill you, right? Then the question remains, how will I fulfil all this without a body? How do we undo the fae's pact?"

Hortencia let go of me completely and took a step back, her right hand still clutching Pythia's.

"The answer is simple," she croaked, beginning to back away from me with her sister.

The motion sent alarm bells ringing. *Is she just going to abandon me now? Tell me to figure it all out by myself, as part of some fifth test?*

"Wait," I said, moving forward.

"Fear not," Hortencia cooed. The twins' steps sped up, even as they continued walking backwards. *Can she sense that they're heading in a direct line for the crater?*

"No, I mean, seriously wait! You're going to fall!"

I lunged to grab the sisters, but by some mysticism, I found myself grasping air instead, even though they were less than a foot in front of me. Then in a sudden jolt, their speed ramped up to a supernatural level and then it was too late. They'd ventured too far. Except they didn't fall.

My heart leaping into my throat, I skidded to a stop in front of them. Through the thick smog, I glimpsed the soles of their feet virtually a centimeter from the edge. All it would take to make them lose balance was a strong gust of wind, yet still they remained facing me, their backs to the sweltering crater.

Before I could utter a word, Hortencia rummaged in her robe pocket and withdrew a round metal pendant. She reached out and pressed it into my hands.

"Keep this," she wheezed amidst the smoke.

As she withdrew her hand, her clothes vanished from her body, rendering her as stark naked as her sister. Then the two, holding hands, whispered in unison like a chant, *"Together we came, together we go. Just you and I, sisters both."*

They turned to face one another, their arms wound around each other's waists, their forms locking together with disturbing symmetry. The next thing I knew, they'd released their balance on the edge and were falling. Falling. Falling. I peered over the edge just in time to glimpse their tightly bound forms making contact with the molten lava. And then they were gone.

BEN

The last thing I'd been expecting was for the oracles to kill themselves. Taking themselves out of the picture to not only keep me alive, but also prevent more disaster in the human world—which the fae had promised to cause if we failed—it was selfless.

Stepping back from the crater as it belched up a spurt of lava, I gazed down at the pendant clasped in my hand. To my surprise, it had popped open, revealing a little compartment within its belly, where lay a key. A tiny silver key.

What is this? Why did she give it to me?

Typical Hortencia. Puzzles, even after her death. She just couldn't help herself. Perhaps it was something that Sherus needed.

Gazing at the crater—now the oracles' grave—one last time, I didn't stick around to see if I could spot their spirits flying out. I hurried back down to the desert.

"Well? What happened?" River and Aisha demanded.

"They're dead."

"What?" River gasped, while Aisha's eyes bulged. "You killed them?"

"No," I said quickly. "They killed themselves. Leapt into the crater."

"Oh, my goodness," Aisha breathed.

"Hortencia gave me this before she left," I said, handing the pendant to Aisha. I wondered if she would have a better idea what it was.

She examined it curiously, yet tentatively, as if expecting it might explode. She picked up the small key. Then she shrugged. "No idea what this is."

"Wh-why would they kill themselves?" River asked, staring at me.

I explained to the girls what happened. By the time I was done their jaws were on the ground.

"So… they weren't that bad after all," River said.

"I guess not," I replied.

There was a span of silence as we exchanged glances.

"So I guess we need to head back to Sherus now," Aisha said, handing the pendant back to me.

I glanced at the letter I still clutched in one hand. Hortencia's last message had disappeared. An unexpected feeling of melancholy washed over me as I stared down at the blank parchment. *The oracles are gone.* It was a shame they had seen no other way than to take their own lives. They could have been infinitely useful to us in this mysterious future she spoke of. I also felt humbled that she had chosen me to impart her final words of wisdom to.

Placing the note on the sand, I pushed it deep, as if in a memorial for Hortencia, a burial that she would never have.

However the world around The Shade would transform in the future, I fully believed that in the short time I'd known her, and the few interactions I'd had with her, she'd made a mark on my character—a mark that would not easily be scrubbed off.

***

Since we still had time, we returned first to the area outside Hortencia's cave—a strange place to return now, knowing that she was gone—in order to fetch the others. When we arrived, our jinn and fae were waiting among the rocks, but everyone else, except for Jeramiah, was nowhere to be seen. Lucas was the first to spot us as we approached.

"Where are the others?" I asked anxiously.

"They finally took your suggestion to leave. They trust you're in safe hands with the jinn."

Good. I was glad they'd gone back. Now there was just River for me to worry about. She and Jeramiah were the only wholly physical creatures remaining with us.

"So, what happened?" Lucas asked, as the rest of the fae— Nolan, Chantel and Marcilla—along with Horatio and the Nasiris gathered round me.

I recounted as briefly as I could what had transpired, and what remained for us to do now. Once all questions were answered, we left the rocks and headed back to the snowy mountain portal.

Even though we were early, somehow I was already expecting Sherus to be waiting there for us. And he was. But I had not been expecting to see an army of fae with him. There must have been over two hundred fae on the icy plateau, lining up in rows, armed with slender bows and arrows, spears and swords, among other weapons.

What on earth is going on here?

As we descended, I caught sight of Sherus. He looked tense as he paced among the rows of fae, barking orders and checking weaponry.

"Hey!" I called, touching down in the snow.

I really did not appreciate the grim expression on his face

after the hell I'd just been through for him.

"So you killed them," he said. Strangely, it was a statement, not a question.

"Uh, they're dead," I replied, frowning at him. "How did you know?"

He reached into a leather pouch fastened to his waist and pulled out a pendant. Identical to the one I held in my palm. His had popped open like mine, too, and a little key rested within it.

Before I could ask, Sherus explained, "These pendants… three were made. One for the oracles, one for the fae, one for the ghouls. The closed metal shells around these silver keys were symbolic of our pact so long as they remained tightly clasped." He paused, clenching his jaw. "I knew you'd managed to end them as soon as my pendant snapped open. And so will the ghouls. Our scouts have already informed us that they are all but deserting The Underworld for battle. Hordes will arrive any moment now."

"Battle?" I asked. "What for?"

"Obviously, the ghouls are not happy that the pact has been broken before we fulfilled their ludicrous demands. They will not let us off easily."

I tensed. "What do you mean? What will they do? Attack and storm your homeland?"

"Attack us, yes. Storm our kingdom, hopefully not." His

eyes left me and wandered across the snowy landscape before returning with a resolute expression. He took the pendant from me. "No matter the repercussions," he said with a heavy sigh, placing the second pendant into his pouch, "this is our fight. You have fulfilled *your* end of the deal, Prince Novak. And now… you are free to leave with what I promised you."

My chest swelled with relief. As soon as Sherus had started talking about the impending battle between the fae and the ghouls, I'd been expecting him to spring on me another hoop I'd have to jump through before he'd allow us to keep our bodies. But Sherus had proven himself to be a man of his word. He might not be at the top of my friends list—or anywhere near it—but I respected and recognized the fact that he had at least some integrity.

I could not bring myself to say thank you, but I bowed my head slightly.

He nodded curtly, then pivoted on his heels, heading back into the midst of his army, where he busied himself again in preparations for the looming attack.

I turned to my companions. Eyeing the line of jinn, I smiled faintly. How ironic it was that, after everything, we had not even needed them for Sherus' task. The oracles had done the job for them… though Sherus didn't need to know that.

Ben

If the ghouls were heading this way, we ought to get a move on. I did not want to get caught up in the crossfire, especially not with River around. We left the fae's plateau and moved to a mountain several miles away, where we could talk without anxiety.

It still hadn't registered in my brain that this was where my journey was supposed to end. My wild, crazy journey that had started the day my father had turned me into a vampire—or even far before that, if you counted my encounter with Basilius.

I kept thinking something else was about to come flying at me. Another blow to return me to my knees, another bombshell to shatter me.

River slid off my back. Standing on my feet to keep her soles from touching the snow, she gazed up at me.

"This... this is it?" she breathed, only half believing it herself.

"I guess so," I said slowly, like I was drugged.

I'd gotten rid of my old infected vampire body, and managed to find a brand-new one—one that would hopefully last me for the rest of my life.

And River and I... we could be together. We could marry.

What more was there to solve?

Yet there was a nagging at the back of my head. A tugging in my chest. That this couldn't be the end, not yet. There was still something I had to accomplish... and as I recalled Sherus' words, I knew what it was.

"... they are all but deserting The Underworld for battle."

Those poor ghosts, cooped up like animals in that ghastly realm. They were doomed to a fate that was probably worse than actual hell.

We, on the other hand... We had jinn with us. We had fae. Both subtle species who could meet the ghouls on their own terms. I'd seen Sherus and his companion chop off ghouls' heads before. Even if there were ghouls who remained in their home to keep watch, we could handle them, couldn't we? We'd leave River and Jeramiah well away from the entrance, and leave a jinni to keep them safe.

I didn't know if such a large-scale evacuation of the ghouls would ever happen again in the future, or had ever happened in history for that matter. After being gifted this fae body, it felt like my responsibility to return for those poor souls we'd left behind.

I surveyed the expectant faces around me. "Before I head back to The Shade, I have some unfinished business to see to. I am not insisting that any of you come with me, though I will appreciate all the help I can get."

River's brows knotted in a frown. "What, Ben?"

A trip down Nightmare Lane.

***

Everyone's faces dropped as I explained what I wanted to do, but not one of them backed out. Not even Lucas.

The jinn vanished us from the mountain peak and transported us to the bank of a swirling lake in the heart of a forest. In the center of the lake was the mouth of the whirlpool. I realized that this was the first time I'd actually seen its exterior. Each time I'd been flown in and out so quickly that I had not gotten a chance to take a proper look at it.

We decided that Nuriya would hide somewhere safe in the forest with River and Jeramiah, because Nuriya was still the weakest of the jinn, being in recovery from that nasty poison bath Cyrus had given her. Once they were gone, the rest of us launched into the air and approached the vortex. We dove through the swirling waters and were soon enshrouded in darkness before being flung out into The Underworld's all-too-familiar entrance cavern.

A horrible sense of déjà vu rolled over me as I played over in my head all the desperate hours I'd spent in here, plotting to escape. But now I was back. *Back with a vengeance.*

I soon spotted six ghouls, perched on some rocks near the entrance. Since we were in our subtle states, they hadn't noticed us yet. Glancing back up at the entrance, I realized they had fixed the net over it, yet we had passed through without noticing. Perhaps the net was only effective with ghosts.

We shot toward the winding canal and wound through it to the cavern that housed the main door to The Underworld. As we drifted through and began scoping out the chambers, it was clear that, although there were some ghouls floating around, none of them looked in any particular urgency to go anywhere, which in all likelihood meant these were the ghouls who had stayed behind, and most of the others had already left.

We gathered together in a shadowy corner and formed a plan for how best to free the ghosts. We couldn't risk getting them into hot water by allowing the ghouls to catch them out of their pools before they ever managed to escape the place.

I suggested that the first thing we had to do was clear the exit. The net had to come down. I assigned the task to a group of five jinn, while the rest of us—armed with swords and spears provided by the jinn—began to approach the pools. Thankfully, there were currently no ghouls in the chamber we were in. Lucas, Marcilla and I dipped into the water of the same pool at once. We sank down and gazed around at the ghosts' fearful faces. It did not help that we were fae—the very creatures who had kidnapped them here in the first place. Even those ghosts I recognized vaguely from my time here—and whom Marcilla must have known well—cowered away from us. It took all that we had to convince them we'd come to help them.

"Ghouls!" Aisha's voice echoed around the chamber from above.

I glided to the surface and poked my head out to see five ghouls had just entered the chamber. They stopped short, shock flashing across their gaunt faces. Aisha and the jinn barely gave them a second's warning. All five ghouls went slamming back against the wall, pinned there by the jinn's magic. Then Aisha rushed over, her blade bared, and dismembered them one by one. As she turned to survey the rest of us, casually brushing aside a strand of hair from her face, she looked like she belonged in a video game.

"Nothing to worry about," she said to me, her tone almost chirpy. "We'll keep watch."

Lucas, Marcilla and I sank into the pool again and I realized that some of the ghosts had also risen to the surface to watch the incident. Now that they had seen one of my companions slaughter those ghouls, it became a much easier task to win their trust and persuade them to come with us.

Soon we had emptied the whole pool and lined them up in a huddle, surrounded by jinn for protection. I caught sight of Nolan and Chantel emerging from the pool next to us, followed by their own crowd of nervous ghosts. I looked toward our jinn. There seemed to be plenty with us to keep watch—especially with Aisha on the patrol—and we needed more help in gathering the ghosts. I picked out several from the crowd, and slowly but surely, we emptied every single pool.

Safi, who had led the jinn who'd parted ways with us to destroy the net, had returned by now, confirming that the net was successfully removed and the ghoul guards all slain.

"Take these ghosts," I said to her. "Escort them through the exit, then return to us for the next batch. And hurry."

Safi nodded before beginning to work with her group to herd the ghosts away.

We, too, needed to hurry.

More ghouls ventured in to disturb us as we continued to move from chamber to chamber, hauling out as many ghosts as we could. But the jinn made sure they didn't come near the ghosts, allowing us to focus on our task of gathering them. Our greatest resistance came from the ghosts themselves. We were moving so slowly due to our efforts to convince even the most stubborn ghosts we were here to help them that I feared we might not even be finished by the time the rest of the ghouls returned. We had to speed up, which—regrettably—meant that those who required persuasion and hesitated at risks started getting left behind.

After emptying the upper levels, we began moving further down. These ghosts, as was to be expected, were ten times more difficult to get through to. Of all the pools, we only managed to salvage twelve ghosts. This number only dwindled further the lower we sank until we were plunged into black. I was sure we had reached the very bottom floor. The jinn had to spark up fires in their palms to give us light.

"Would be a miracle if we rescued a single person from here," Lucas murmured. His face looked strained as his eyes roamed the deathly-still ponds.

As I looked at my uncle, I took a moment to appreciate the fact that he'd been willing to come down here to help us. After all those years of hell, he shouldn't have wanted to come within a thousand miles of here.

Then, as the jinn began to mutter about our job being done, a thought struck me. "Where is The Necropolis?"

Lucas's eyes widened. "Uh... further down still, I guess."

"You have never seen the place."

Lucas shook his head, shuddering slightly.

"How do we know it even exists?" I asked.

"It exists," Marcilla spoke up, half scoffing. "Where else would the ghouls throw out the motionless ghosts?"

I paused, running my tongue over my lower lip.

"What are you thinking?" Aisha asked, scrutinizing my face as she leaned on her bloodied sword.

"I'm thinking that we're here now, and will likely—and hopefully—never be here again... I would like to see The Necropolis for myself." If not now, I'd wonder for the rest of my life what it really was.

"Are you serious?" Chantel gasped.

I nodded grimly.

"I'll come with you," Aisha offered.

"I'll come, too," Horatio blurted, a little too quickly after Aisha. They slanted glances at each other at the same time, before meeting each other's gaze and averting their attention awkwardly.

"And I... will *not* come with you this time," Lucas said, grimacing. I certainly could not blame him for having drawn the line here.

To my surprise, Nolan did put himself forward, much to his wife's chagrin.

When we had no more offers after his, I cleared my throat. "All right… Let's do this."

BEΠ

We sank through the floor—deeper than we'd ever sunk before—and passed through dozens of feet of solid rock. When we finally emerged on the other side, a faint moaning sound met my ears, like high wind against a loose window. Sprawling beneath us was a most bizarre sight. I had been expecting perhaps another chamber—an enormous one to house all the faded ghosts. Instead what I saw was a sea of graves spread out over rolling hills. Strangely, the ground was soil rather than the stone I'd been accustomed to in this place, and gaping dirt holes had been dug in front of each gravestone, none of them covered over. The ceiling was jagged with rocks, and now that I looked up at it, I realized the source of the pale blue light cast down over the landscape. Hordes of swarming glow worms. At least, I assumed they were glow worms. They were some type of insect and their bodies were luminous.

"Whoa," Nolan breathed.

We lowered closer to the gravestones. They were all black and roughly cut, as if no thought had been put into them other than to mark where one grave ended and another started. And the holes themselves… I crept closer still and soon realized that they were not empty. They contained ghosts. I had not been able to spot them from afar, because they were cast in shadow; their forms no longer possessed even the slightest bit of aura. They were as dark as the soil that surrounded them.

So this is what a dead ghost looks like. I was still trying to wrap my mind around the notion when Horatio whispered, "What *is* that sound?"

Leaving the edge of the grave we had been staring down into, we rose up again, straining to make out where the noise was coming from. It sounded like it was drifting from the other side of the hills. We began flying toward it and the closer we got, the more I couldn't shake the feeling that it was not howling wind—*where would wind come from anyway in this place, genius?*

No. It sounded more like… some kind of ghastly singing. And it was getting louder.

Aisha stopped short and pointed to a cluster of gravestones to our far right.

"There," she whispered.

I held my breath as I spotted something moving. A tall, and oddly wide, figure was gliding in and out between the gravestones. My first assumption was that it was a ghoul, but its shape was all wrong. It looked almost... overweight. Of all the ghouls I'd had the misfortune of coming across, I'd never seen a single one that did not look painfully emaciated.

"It's a ghoul," Horatio whispered, to my confusion.

"What?" I breathed, straining my eyes.

As the supposed ghoul drew nearer, I realized Horatio was right. It shared every other trait of a ghoul: skin so thin it revealed the cold blue veins beneath it; jagged, shark-like teeth; tufts of hair on a balding skull; glowing eyes; gnarled hands with sharp black nails. I could go on. This was a ghoul—an obese, female ghoul. And now that I looked closer still, I realized she was wearing something on her head. A tiara made of decayed teeth.

"This must be the queen," Horatio whispered.

I had wondered about the hierarchy of ghouls, whether they even had one. Now I had my answer.

The queen's face was paunchy, rolls of fat hanging beneath her chin, as she bumped a heavy hand along the tops of the gravestones. She appeared to be wandering aimlessly, her jaws open as she continued to emit that hideous wailing sound. *Even worse than my country singing.*

We hovered in the shadows, transfixed, even as she began to move closer to us. Then she halted and stooped to the ground. Craning my neck, I realized she was bending right over one of the graves. When she rose again, she was holding a dead ghost by the neck.

What happened next was even creepier than her singing. Her jaws extended and her folds of belly flab shook as she inhaled deeply. The next thing I knew, she'd sucked the ghost's head into her mouth, then the body, the legs, until the ghost was gone.

What the...

The queen belched, her cheeks bloating. I thought for a moment that she was going to throw up but then, opening her mouth again, she continued to inflict her singing on us.

She'd just eaten a ghost.

I looked to my companions, wondering if they had seen what I'd just seen; from the looks on their faces, they had.

Did this queen live upstairs? Or was The Necropolis her quarters? Did she stay down here all day, snacking on ghosts, while her citizens kept the graves constantly refilled with new dead arrivals?

"Why is she so stout?" Nolan whispered.

Fair point. I would've thought that ghosts would make for

rather a light diet.

"Oh, ghosts can't be all she consumes," Horatio whispered. "I'm guessing she inhales them for their memories. Her actual diet must be just like the others'—real corpses… I think we should move," he added tensely.

He was right. She was nearing too close for comfort now.

"Why should we move?" Aisha whispered, clutching the hilt of her sword.

I should have seen it coming. Before any of us could stop her, she left our hiding place and shot toward the queen, wielding her blade.

The queen's whining morphed into a howl as she spotted the jinni. And then she disappeared before Aisha could reach her.

Aisha cursed beneath her breath, returning to us. We gazed around the now deserted graveyard. The silence was far more chilling than the ghoul's singing. We had no idea where she was.

"Okay," Nolan breathed. "I think we should leave."

"Agreed," I muttered. It was pointless—and now potentially dangerous—to spend more time here. Besides, we'd seen all there was to see: a sprawling underground graveyard… a memory buffet.

We made our way around a cluster of headstones before

lifting into the air. We had almost reached the ceiling when Nolan yelped behind me. I whirled around to see the ghoul queen clutching Nolan by the throat. What had possessed him to remain in his physical form even as we traveled was beyond me. Her mustard eyes glowed maliciously as her black claws pressed against Nolan's skin.

Horatio and Aisha had already leapt forward before I could, but not before the queen had punctured Nolan's throat—too deep, I feared. Before the jinn could catch her, she let go of Nolan and again vanished. Nolan, apparently unable to keep himself mid-air, went tumbling to the ground. I caught up with him just in time before his body made contact. My stomach tensed at the sight of his puncture wounds and how much blood was flowing from them.

"Let's get out of here!" I hissed.

Before the invisible queen could attempt to launch another attack, the jinn transported us away. When we stopped moving, we were back in the dark chamber where we'd left the others.

On seeing her husband, Chantel shrieked and hurried toward us. She took him from my hands and laid him down on the floor, gasping at his wounds.

"It's all right," Horatio said, pushing her aside. "I can heal him."

Thank God for that. My gut had already been twisting up in knots at the thought of being responsible for his death. If I hadn't suggested we go down there, Nolan never would have gone in a million years.

Lucas and Marcilla approached me while Horatio bent over Nolan. But I was too tense to talk until Horatio had managed to stem the bleeding by some mysticism. Aisha in the meantime, recounted our brief foray downstairs.

When Nolan eventually sat up, he was clutching his neck and wincing. He uttered what I was sure was a profanity in French. Then he fixed his eyes on me, shaking his head. "That was just... too much."

I agreed. The Necropolis and its repugnant overlady were a level of bizarre that sent even my inured mind into a tailspin.

Some stones were best left unturned.

***

The jinn returned us to the main entrance of The Underworld—the heavy oaken door. Here we found the group of jinn who'd been put in charge of transporting the remaining ghosts safely through the portal.

"So are all the ghosts safe? Where did you put them?" I asked before they could bombard us with their own questions.

"They're safe," Safi replied, looking relieved to see us. "We just took them out through the whirlpool. They did not wait around; they must have all cleared off by now."

"All right," I said, breathing out. "Let's leave."

We hurried to the main entrance chamber where the corpses of the guards floated in the water. I wondered if ghouls collected dead relics of their own kind... or even ate them. I wouldn't put anything past these demons.

Once we passed through the portal, it was a relief to soar out the other end. Sun shone down on us, hitting my skin and sending warmth rolling through my body. Crossing the lake, we touched down on the bank and began yelling for Jeramiah, River and Nuriya, wherever they'd been hiding. To my relief, nothing had gone wrong with them. Nuriya appeared with them after a minute; all three looked perfectly unruffled. I would have been interested to witness the conversation that had gone on between Jeramiah and River while I was gone; I was sure that she would have had a thing or two to say to him.

River moved to me and pulled me close. "Glad you didn't kill yourself again," she murmured, pressing her lips to mine.

"I'm glad too," I said, before recounting what had happened to River and Nuriya, while Lucas conversed with his son.

Once we were done with our explanations, we all exchanged glances. It was clear from everyone's expressions that all we wanted now was rest. Peace. The Shade.

BEN

As we arrived outside our island's boundary, warmth billowed in my heart. I was beaming from ear to ear. I was home. And hopefully, I'd never be forced to leave it again.

First we had to catch the attention of one of the witches to let us inside, something that wasn't difficult to do. I guessed my parents must've told the witches to keep an especially sharp ear out in anticipation of our return. I wasn't sure if the jinn might have been able to break through it, but I wasn't about to ask them to try. Something told me that the witches would not take too kindly to learning that their spell had been knocked out by our jinn, whom they already held an innate hostility toward.

Corrine arrived quickly, her eyes sweeping over the jinn and fae. She performed her regular checks on all of us—though I couldn't help but notice she spent longer on each of the jinn—before allowing us in.

As we descended to the forest ground, Corrine gushed over how relieved she was that we had returned safely. Then she asked in a low voice, "Do you think the jinn will be staying?"

"I think so," I replied. "At least for a while... maybe permanently."

My heart felt like it would burst with happiness as our feet landed on the soil. There were so many people I wanted to see now that I was back. But first, I needed to visit my parents. I asked Corrine to fix somewhere for the jinn to rest, as well as offer them refreshments, before I raced with River up to the Residences. I had intended to head straight for Vivienne and Xavier's apartment, which was where my parents had been staying, but passing my parents' tree, we found ourselves gazing up at a brand-new penthouse, fully restored to its former glory. The witches must have worked on it since we'd been gone.

We hurried up to the front door, where I knocked hard. It was my mother who opened the door.

Joy and trepidation filled her expression at once, though the latter I quickly ended. "We did it," I said before she could ask. "We completed Sherus' task." *Among other things...*

"Oh, thank God!" She pulled me into her arms, her cheek squished against mine as she held me close. My father arrived behind her and pulled me in for a hug once my mother had moved on to embrace River. Then my sister rushed out.

"You did it!" she squealed, colliding with me before wrapping her arms around my waist.

"Come in," my mother said, pulling us inside.

Vivienne, Xavier and my baby cousin were here too. I hugged my aunt and uncle before leaning down to kiss the baby's forehead. *I never could have done* that *as a vampire.*

"Are you hungry?" my mom asked River and me.

"Yes," River said. I could only imagine how hungry and thirsty she must be—I doubted she had eaten for at least a day. I was about to shake my head when for the first time I realized I was actually hungry. Really hungry. I didn't even know if fae could eat normal food. *If not normal food, then what?* I'd gotten so habituated as a vampire to my body rejecting everything other than human blood, the thought that I might be able to eat real food again was beyond exciting.

We headed into the kitchen and sat down at the table.

"I made macaroni and cheese casserole less than an hour ago," my aunt offered. "It's still hot in my oven. It'll be faster if I fetch that than your mom making something new."

Xavier offered to fetch it, and in the meantime, River and I chugged down glasses of water while everyone bombarded us with questions. When Xavier returned with the dish, a delicious smell filled the room. My mouth salivated. I'd practically forgotten what food tasted like. As I spooned the first bite into my mouth, relief rushed through me. It didn't taste like cardboard. It tasted like my aunt's scrumptious cooking. I'd never thought I could appreciate casserole as much as I did then. I relished every texture, tasted every herb and spice. As hungry as I was, I chewed slowly, not wanting to rush the flavors swimming on my tongue.

I glanced up at River and my family to see that they were watching me.

"Well, one piggy sure is enjoying himself," Rose commented, grinning.

I grinned back.

I realized as I munched that every part of my life would be enhanced from now on. It seemed I, like almost everyone else on the planet, had to be deprived of something before I could truly appreciate it. And appreciate I would; I vowed I wouldn't let a day go past without feeling gratitude for every aspect of my life. From the people I loved, to the food on my plate, to the sand beneath my feet.

For dessert, my mother announced chocolate cake and homemade berry ice cream—made from berries plucked from The Shade's own forests. Once River and I had finished that, we leaned back in our chairs, looking at each other with satisfied smiles.

My mother could hardly keep her hands off me throughout the meal. She'd been sitting next to me, reaching out and touching my hair or arm every few minutes, as if to reassure herself that I was still real. Still here. Still solid. I smiled at her now, and kissed her cheek. "It's okay, Mom," I said to her. "I'm here."

She gave me a teary smile, and I could see how much she appreciated my words. Then she addressed my sister. "Rose, can you go fetch River's family? Nadia's been as anxious as me."

"Sure." Rose got up and sped out of the apartment.

We shifted to the living room and continued recounting everything that had happened since we had last seen them. Then Rose returned with Nadia and River's three siblings. They had a gushy reunion before Nadia came to greet me.

They settled down with us, and we talked for hours, until River could no longer hide her sleepiness. Her head began to nod on my shoulder. Truth be told, I was feeling exhausted too. I couldn't remember the last time I'd slept properly. And the huge meal we had just eaten did not help.

"River and I should get some sleep," I said, bracing River's shoulder gently with my palm.

"The apartment is set up like it was before the fire," my mother said. "Even your old room."

We bade everyone good night before I carried River to where my old bedroom had been. A double bed was in here now.

As I stepped inside with River and closed the door, I was fully aware that finally, we had time alone. But ironically, as I laid River down on the mattress and we curled up together beneath the covers... we really did just sleep.

Ben

When I woke hours later, I felt bewildered as to where I was. I couldn't remember the last time I'd slept in a soft bed, much less with River beside me. My stomach filled with an instinctive dread, a dread I'd been accustomed to waking up with ever since I had turned into a vampire. It took me several moments to remember the reality.

I had reached the end of the tunnel. I was out. Free. Back home.

All was well.

River was still fast asleep in my arms, her right cheek pressed against my chest. Grazing my lips over her forehead, I took a moment to admire her before gently detaching myself and sliding out of bed.

As my feet touched down on the soft carpet and I gazed at my familiar surroundings, I wasn't sure I'd ever felt so alive. So excited for the day ahead. So happy.

I moved to the window and looked out. This bedroom had a magnificent view of the back of the forest and the waves beyond. I gazed out toward The Shade's boundary to see that the sun had risen beyond it. I glanced at the clock. Six AM. I drew open the window and inhaled the fresh air. A breeze ventured in, carrying with it the fragrant scent of damp soil. Pearls of water dripped from the redwood branches by my window. It had rained overnight. I breathed in deeply, filling my lungs with the pure air.

Then I headed to the bathroom, where I brushed my teeth and took a shower. Gazing at myself in the mirror, I wasn't sure how long it would take me to get used to seeing myself in this body. Though I looked mostly the same—my eye and hair color, and the general structure of my face—my features seemed to be slightly sharper in appearance. The tips of my ears for example, were more slanted... rather elvish. And then there was the fact that my body literally glowed. It had a faint, almost golden aura to it. I smiled to myself, remembering how River had mistaken me for an angel.

Once I had dressed in jeans and a T-shirt—which my mother had thoughtfully left for me in the closet—I glanced at River again. She had turned over, her face buried in a pillow. Still fast asleep. That suited me fine. I had things that I wanted to do while she was still asleep.

I needed to have another discussion with my parents, but first, I needed to talk to River's mother. Properly.

Leaving my bedroom, I found my mother roaming around in her nightdress. I wondered if she had gotten even a wink of sleep, or whether my return had made her buzz too much. I hugged her good morning.

"I need to go out for a while," I said, drinking down some water. "I should be back within an hour. And then I need to talk to you and Dad."

"Okay," she said, eyeing me curiously. She was obviously wondering where I was heading off to, but didn't ask. She would find out soon enough…

I left the apartment and descended in the elevator, even as I reminded myself that I could just fly… but I'd had enough of drifting for a lifetime. I wanted to enjoy the walk through the forest to the Vale, feel the ground beneath my feet.

The town was still quiet when I reached it. Beautifully quiet. I passed the gushing fountains in the cobblestone square before heading down River's road. I had considered that River's mom might still be asleep at this time, but if Nadia was anything like my mom, she would in all likelihood be up.

I was right. Pressing my ear against the front door of their townhouse, I heard talking from inside. It sounded like Nadia and Jamil.

Standing up straight, I cleared my throat, feeling suddenly nervous. I reached out and rapped on the door. The conversation faded and footsteps approached the door. It swung open to reveal Nadia standing in the doorway. Her face lit up as she laid eyes on me.

"Ben!" she exclaimed, opening the door wider. "Come in, come in. Where's River?"

I stepped inside. "She's still sleeping."

I followed her through to the kitchen, where Jamil was sitting, sipping from a glass of orange juice. He stood up and shook my hand, smiling broadly.

I sat with them at the table, both of them eyeing me curiously.

I cleared my throat, feeling on edge... and incredibly exposed. *Just get on with it. God knows you've had to do harder things than this in the past year.*

Forcing myself to maintain steady eye contact with Nadia, I confessed, "I'm in love with your daughter."

Warmth rose in Nadia's cheeks, encouraging me to go on.

"I wish to marry her. In fact, I have already proposed to her. I don't believe River had a chance to tell you before we left; and I hope you'll excuse me for not getting your permission first."

I could see Nadia's full set of front teeth through her beaming smile. Tears glistened in her eyes. She glanced at her son, who was also smiling.

She stood up, and pulled me into a hug, kissing my cheek. "All is excused," she said, her eyes twinkling. "The happiest I have ever seen my daughter is when she's with you. You have my blessing, Ben, from the very bottom of my heart."

"Thank you," I said, breathing an internal sigh of relief. I wasn't sure why I had been so anxious. Maybe it was because this was all such unknown territory for me. I'd had a number of girlfriends before River, but I'd never gotten anywhere close to even thinking about marriage in a distant future. Proposing to River, however, had felt so natural that it had slipped from my lips before I'd even fully thought it through.

Jamil pulled me into a hug and clapped me on the back. "And the unhappiest I've ever seen my sister is when you were away."

My heart soaring, I thanked them both once again, before leaving the townhouse. I raced back through the forest to my parents' apartment. The door was unlocked, and the kitchen and living room were empty as I strolled in.

"Mom?" I called softly, still not wanting to wake River in case she was still asleep. "Dad?"

The door to my father's study opened. He stepped out and beckoned me inside. I walked in to find my mother sitting at my father's desk along with Jeriad.

"Would you prefer to converse alone with your son?" Jeriad asked my parents, always the gentleman.

"We would, actually, Jeriad," my father replied. "I'm sorry; if you could just wait in the living room we'll be with you shortly."

"Certainly," Jeriad said, strolling out of the room.

Alone with my parents, I took a seat in Jeriad's chair across my father's large wooden desk. This desk... This room... A wave of nostalgia rolled over me. Standing in this room and writing a hurried note was one of the last memories I had of this island before leaving in the submarine all those months ago. I remembered how much it had killed me to write it; I'd known how much pain it would cause my family to leave. When I'd made that decision, I never could have imagined in a billion years what a ride I was about to go on.

"How are you feeling?" My father smiled, looking me over. It must have been so strange for my parents to have their son leave and return months later as an entirely different species.

"Better than I've ever felt," I replied. "I just went to see River's mother, actually." I paused, wetting my lower lip. "I asked her for permission to marry River."

My mother positively squealed as she leapt from her chair and smothered me in a hug.

I guess that's a sign of approval...

"Oh, Ben," she half sobbed, half laughed.

I checked my father for a reaction. His smile had broadened, and he was eyeing my mother in amusement.

"It seems that your mother is not going to give River the tough time that I gave Caleb," he said to me.

"Why would I give River a tough time?" my mother shot back. "I couldn't imagine a better match for our son." Her green eyes gazed into mine. "I've seen how much she is willing to sacrifice for you. She loves you, truly, Ben."

I nodded, even as my throat tightened a little. "I know she does," I managed. "As I love her."

My mother drew away to allow my father to approach. He planted his hands on my shoulders and looked me straight in the eye, still a hint of amusement playing across his face. I didn't get the impression that any of this had come as a surprise to him at all.

"So... you think you're ready for married life, huh, son?"

I grinned. "I'm ready for any life with River."

He nodded approvingly. "I can see that." He withdrew his hands and stood up straight, looking down at me as I remained seated. "Well, I may not break out in tears like your mother, but trust that I'm just as thrilled as her. River is a strong, courageous young woman. A woman deserving of a Novak... And I recognize happiness in my children when I see it."

My mother slipped her arm around my father's waist, resting her head against him as she looked down at me, still glowing. "With you married, that will mean both of my babies have flown from the nest... both around the ripe old age of eighteen."

"The same age you got married," I reminded her.

She nodded. "Guess it runs in the family."

"You know, it's a funny coincidence," my father said thoughtfully, changing the subject. He and my mom retook their seats. "You know what Jeriad was just in here talking to us about?"

"What?" I asked, leaning forward.

"He was just telling us that in recent weeks, a number of dragons have proposed to their girlfriends. And while we were away, the dragons started to discuss wedding arrangements." He paused. "First, how soon do you want to get married?"

I hadn't thought about a date. "Uh... I haven't discussed it with River yet... as you can imagine." I smirked. "We haven't exactly been rich with time. But if it was up to me, it would be as soon as possible."

My father smiled, and stroked his jaw. "Well, back to the

dragons… They all wish to return to their home country to get married, The Hearthlands. Now, I don't know how you feel about a joint wedding, and I've never been to The Hearthlands myself so I don't know what it's like, but from what Rose has told us it's quite a magnificent place. The dragons plan to return as early as tomorrow with their fiancées, and as I understand it, the grand wedding will take place a couple of days after that."

My mind lit up with excitement. A wedding in The Hearthlands. That sounded pretty epic. I imagined that River would be thrilled at the idea. "Let me talk to her," I said, jumping from my seat. "I'll let you know."

"Yes," my mom added, "Because if we are going to tag along, we have a lot of arrangements to make in a very short time." She turned to my father. "We'll also need to be sure Jeriad doesn't mind, though I can't imagine he'd object."

I left the room and was about to rush straight for River's door when I paused. *Wait, not yet. I'm not ready.*

As my parents came out of the study and began conversing with Jeriad again, I told them, "I forgot that there's something I need to do first."

With that, I hurried back out of the apartment. I wanted to do things in a little more orthodox fashion this time… and that would involve seeking out the best jeweler our island had to offer: Corrine.

RIVER

My eyelids felt like lead as they lifted. I stretched out, expecting to feel Ben next to me, but he wasn't. I got out of bed and, after brushing my teeth and sweeping my hair into a ponytail, I left the room and wandered through the apartment. It appeared empty. I padded into the kitchen to get some water and munch on an apple. I noticed a note on the table:

"Come outside."

Is that Ben's handwriting? I wasn't sure if I had ever seen his real handwriting. The last note he'd left me had been written with Shadow's paw.

I finished my apple quickly and walked outside the front door. On the doorstep was another note, this time drawn with chalk.

"Keep going."

Next to the writing was an arrow, pointing to the elevator.

Frowning, I stepped inside the elevator and descended to the ground. Here, yet another arrow had been drawn into the soil, pointing to my right.

Rather amused by now, I began wandering through the forest, keeping my eyes on the ground for the next direction. Every few yards, there was an arrow pointing ahead, reassuring me that I had not lost this mysterious trail.

I soon realized that I was heading toward the mountains. The trees began to thin, and I neared the edge of the forest. Soon I had arrived in the large clearing in front of the main entrance to the Black Heights. My ever-conscientious sign-drawer had left more arrows, leading me diagonally across the clearing to the stone steps that led up the mountainside. I mounted them and climbed swiftly. By the time I reached the top of the stairs and staggered forward onto a grassy plain, the muscles in my legs were aching. It was times like this when I became aware that half of me was still very much human.

The view up here was out of this world. But I did not linger long on the stunning landscape or the glistening waves surrounding it. I looked back down at the ground, searching for my next instruction. I found it to my left, pointing to yet another flight of stairs that would lead me to an even higher plateau. Arriving at the top, I stopped short as I laid eyes on the plateau. Smack-bang in the center of it was... *a sauna?*

What the heck is Ben playing at?

A smile was already splitting my face as I approached the wooden structure, but when I noticed Ben through the glass, I burst out laughing.

His hair slicked back, his upper chest exposed, he was wearing a virgin-white bathrobe. He was leaning back casually, one arm resting over the backrest of the bench. Noticing me, he raised one brow, holding a glass of what looked like pineapple juice and raising it, as if to say "cheers".

With the heavenly view sprawled out all around us, it felt like I'd just walked onto the set of a sauna commercial. The fact that Ben literally emitted a golden-yellow aura didn't help either.

"Ben!" I gasped, almost crying with laughter. "What the heck?"

Setting aside his glass, he stood up and opened the glass door to let me in.

I stared at him, still laughing. "What is all this?"

He just smiled. Wordlessly, he closed the door behind us before taking my hands and seating me on the bench.

Wow, it was warm in here. I felt my cheeks flushing already.

Ben sat down beside me, retaking his glass of juice and sipping before saying in a light, pleasant voice, "We first met in one of these. Don't you remember?"

Finally managing to stop giggling, I thought back to the first time I had ever met my now-fiancé. Indeed, it had been in a sauna. Back in The Oasis. At that time, I had known him only as Joseph. Jeramiah had wanted him to half-turn me, but he'd refused. He'd darted out of that sauna the moment he saw me. How long ago that seemed now...

"Yes," I said. "Of course I remember."

"Then," he said, "don't you think that this is all... rather appropriate?"

"Appropriate for what?" I half laughed, half frowned.

He set down his pineapple juice again. Then he stood up, tightening the rope of his bathrobe around his waist before lowering himself to the floor... on one knee. His right hand delved into the pocket of his bathrobe, and when he withdrew it, he was holding a round box the color and texture of pearl. My breath hitched as he opened it to reveal an even more beautiful object. A delicate silver ring, crowned with a gemstone the color of brilliant turquoise. The color of my eyes.

His face had gone serious now. He cleared his throat and said in a low voice, "Will you marry me, River Giovanni?"

Even as I felt breathless, I couldn't help but grin. "Again?"

I whispered.

His lips curved in a smile. "Again."

Sliding off the bench, I sank down to his level and flung my arms around his neck. "I'll marry you a hundred times, Ben," I said, before pushing my lips to his.

His smile split our kiss. His hands slid up my shoulders and pushed me backward. "Wait, River," he said, his face deadpan as he reached for my ring finger. "You're doing it the wrong way round. I'm supposed to put my ring on you first."

"Says the man who proposed before he had a ring." I smirked. "I think we should just admit we've botched this whole engagement thing. I'm simply happy I'm not betrothed to a ghost."

Ben took my hand and placed the ring on my finger all the same. I gazed down at it, admiring the way it shimmered against the aura of Ben's body. Then he pulled me up and we stood side by side. He leaned down, allowing us to lock lips again in a long, tender kiss.

"Mmm," I murmured, as we surfaced for breath. "You taste like pineapple juice."

Ben raised a brow. "And what's more sexy than that?"

"A hunky fairy in a virgin-white bathrobe."

Ben snorted. "Then I couldn't have pulled this off better, could I?"

We moved to sit down on the bench again, but I pushed open the door first to let in the breeze. Then I sat next to him, taking his hand and twining my fingers through his.

"Thank you, Ben," I whispered, glancing again at my sparkling ring.

He brushed his lips against the top of my head and I nestled closer against him. Then we both gazed out at the beauty of the island and sank into comfortable silence. The redwoods swayed gently in the breeze, and the lakes sparkled. Rolling meadows of flowers flowed into fields of vegetables and grain. I could lose myself forever in this view.

"So," I murmured, "will we get married in this sauna too?"

"That wouldn't be very creative of me," Ben said. "I actually had a different idea for the location of our wedding. But it kind of depends on when you want to get married."

I looked up at him. "When? Well, when would you want to get married?"

"As soon as you want to," he replied.

"What if I said I wanted to marry you right here, right now?"

"I would ask if you could wait a day or two, when we could join The Shade's dragons and their mates in a grand wedding ceremony in The Hearthlands."

I wondered if this was another joke. "The Hearthlands? Are you serious?"

"Yes," he said. He stood up and gazed down at me, touching my cheek. "I'm quite serious."

Oh, my. Is that even a question? "Yes!" I exclaimed, jumping up in excitement. The little girl inside of me was squealing.

He smiled broadly as he braced my shoulders. "Then we should start getting ready, future princess of The Shade."

DEREK

Sofia and I had very little time for preparations once we'd received confirmation from Jeriad that Ben and River were welcome to accompany them, and Ben confirmed they were both happy to take part in a joint wedding.

We made a trip around the island inviting people personally; it was something we wanted to do, given that it was our son's wedding. Two other couples also decided to join the bandwagon and tie the knot at the same time: Helena and Matteo, and Micah and Kira.

And then there remained only one person I had left to speak to.

My brother.

I still hadn't had much time to speak to him—and absolutely no time alone. Even though we'd gone together to The Dunes and then Hortencia's cave, Lucas hadn't been around much since, being a fae, he'd been helping Ben and the jinn much of the time.

It was time that I talked to him man to man. Brother to brother. Although I was dreading it, there would be no better moment than now.

I told Sofia where I was going before heading off to look for him. I spotted him eventually on the beach near the Port. He was sitting with Jeramiah and talking, their feet submerged in the water.

I felt hesitant to approach, but forced myself to interrupt by arriving at their side and clearing my throat.

Lucas's eyes widened in surprise as he looked up to see that it was me.

I turned my focus to Jeramiah. "If you don't mind, I would like a few words with your father."

Jeramiah nodded curtly. Lucas stood up, his height just less than mine. I found it hard to hold his gaze for long and, it seemed, so did he. We both looked away in opposite directions even as we began to walk together along the beach, away from Jeramiah.

When he made no move to say anything after about a minute, I attempted to break the ice. "Thank you for helping my son."

Still looking at the sand, Lucas murmured with a dismissive shrug, "I owed him."

I swallowed. *What do I talk about with him?* I had decided to invite him to the wedding, but that wasn't what I'd really come here for.

Trying to converse with Lucas felt more uncomfortable than attempting to strike up a conversation with a complete stranger. At least a stranger shared no past with you. No hateful, envious past.

To my relief, Lucas took his turn in saying something. "You should, uh," he began, wetting his lower lip. "You should be proud of your son."

I stopped walking, causing him to stop too. I felt the urge to look him in the eyes. His cold blue irises that matched my own locked with mine.

"I am very proud of him," I said, steadily holding his gaze. *And I wish I could return the compliment to your son.* Jeramiah was not inherently bad, but he still had a lot of work to do on his character, a lot of strength to build up if he wanted to be anywhere near the man my son had become.

Though now that Lucas was back, hopefully a changed man, maybe he would become the role model Jeramiah had always hoped for.

I hesitated before speaking again. "Did you really never

tell a soul about Jeramiah?" I asked. "Not even Father?"

He swallowed, and I lost his eye contact again. He grimaced as he gazed out toward the ocean. He shook his head.

"Why?" I prodded.

"Isn't that obvious?"

"I can't say that anything about you is obvious to me anymore."

Lucas paused, his eyes darting toward me again. From the look on his face, he took that as a compliment. And I guessed it was.

"I wasn't proud of what I did, Derek," he said darkly.

"You did a lot of things that you weren't proud of—or at least, shouldn't have been proud of—but that never usually stopped you from boasting." I wondered if I might have pushed the boundary a little too far with this remark as his jaw tensed. I was expecting the old, prickly Lucas to rise to the surface. But then his jaw loosened.

He heaved a sigh. "Yes. But some more than others."

"What other secrets have you been keeping?" I forged on.

At this, he looked at me curiously, almost half amused. His lips curled. "What business is that of yours?"

"Uh, well, after what your son attempted to do to us, it would be good to know if there are any other skeletons in your closet who might come back to haunt us."

His eyes darkened, then he shook his head again. "You've seen the worst of it." We fell into silence as we continued to walk. Then he murmured, "So you finally got your little twig in the end."

Little twig. It took me a few moments to remember that was what he used to call Sofia. "Yeah…" I said. "You don't need to call her that anymore. She's no longer the wide-eyed seventeen-year-old you swept up from a beach, I assure you that much."

"Oh, I can see that she's not," he said, a little quickly. He almost seemed… worried that he might've offended me. I realized that he'd spoken with tongue in cheek. I was once again struck by how in tune he seemed to those around him, no longer in his little narcissistic bubble he used to float around in day and night.

"I would like to apologize to her," he said, after yet another pause. His voice sounded a little unsteady as he added, "Properly."

"I'm sure there will be ample opportunity for that," I said.

Sofia was a forgiving person. It just was not in her nature to hold a grudge. No matter what atrocities a person might have committed in the past, if she saw genuine repentance in a person's eyes, she was the first to give them a second chance. I found myself wondering whether Lucas had feelings for her. I had thought at the time that his pull to her was just lust, as it was with all the other young women who had the misfortune of crossing paths with him. Now that I thought back over my brother's life, I could not summon a single instance when he'd had an actual girlfriend. Claudia was probably the closest he'd come to one, though theirs was anything but an actual relationship. They had been on and off for centuries, but it had been no secret to anyone on the island that they met only for one thing.

As we reached the end of this stretch of beach and turned around, I glanced at my brother thoughtfully while he looked straight ahead. For the first time, it really hit me in a way that it never had before: *Has he really never fallen in love?* The only person I'd ever known him to be in love with was himself. Maybe Vivienne shared a piece of his heart... though not a large piece, since Lucas had gone along with my father's plan to bundle her off to Borys Maslen. Lucas couldn't have loved Jeramiah or his mother much either, or he would not have abandoned them so callously. Both of these incidents had taken place even before he became a vampire—he had been a mere human then. It was as if he'd been born with these cold, harsh traits. Could I really blame all of this on my father?

It had been my very own Sofia who had drilled into my mindset that we could control ourselves, that we were all responsible. Even those infected with the dark disease of vampirism. That was how she'd gotten me to change. The thought brought me full circle and made me recall Claudia's original point: Lucas had never gotten any good loving, like I had. He had never met a woman who could change him the way I had met Sofia. Maybe one of the reasons he'd been so drawn to her was because he sensed her goodness, but he hadn't known how to control his nature around her for him to even have a fighting chance of winning her over.

I pulled myself out of my reverie, wondering if I really ought to say what I was tempted to say next.

"You know, I, uh..." I paused as he glanced up at me. I thought to phrase it a different way. "There are a lot of new folks on the island. New since you left, that is... You might be able to find a little twig of your own some day."

I was relieved when Lucas' lips curved. He narrowed his eyes on me slightly. "Whatever might happen," he said in a low voice, "I won't need the assistance of a little brother."

Little brother. That was when it struck me. A sly smile spread across my face at the realization. "You do realize that I am no longer your younger brother. I'm your *older* brother now."

Lucas blinked as it sank in. "How old are you?" he shot back, rather aggressively compared to the way he'd spoken his previous sentence.

"In terms of physical age, I'm pushing twenty-five."

He looked wounded.

"Well, then," he muttered, "it looks like I'll have to spend the next few years as a human..."

"That's a war that could get dangerous," I remarked. "Before we knew it, we'd both be old men."

Lucas smirked. Then, running a hand through his hair, he heaved a sigh. "But seriously, Derek. Hooking up with a girl is really, *really* the last thing on my mind. I've missed out on my son's whole life. I suspect that he will occupy much of my time in the foreseeable future. In fact, he would like us to make a trip to his mother's grave, as soon as I feel ready."

That was fair enough. Though I was sure that with time, some female on this island would catch Lucas' eye—he was only a man, after all. And when it did happen, he had better end up treating her right... or he'd have his older brother to answer to.

Something told me, however, that he would. Something had changed in him, seemingly permanently.

Those ghouls really should charge for their service. Ghoul rehab. Guaranteed results for the assholes in your family.

As Lucas and I began to near Jeramiah, who was still sitting on the same patch of sand, I remembered what had triggered me to seek out my brother in the first place.

"Lucas," I said, stopping. He stopped and looked at me. "I actually came to ask whether you would like to attend

Ben's wedding. Your son is invited too."

Lucas' eyes widened a little. He hesitated, then said, "I... I would be honored to."

A smile spread across my lips. For the first time in my entire life, I actually almost felt like hugging my brother... almost. We sufficed with a handshake instead, but it was the steadiest, firmest handshake we'd ever shared.

BEN

I was pleased that River had enjoyed my second proposal so much. The idea had occurred to me while I'd been on my way to the Sanctuary to request Corrine's help in preparing a suitable ring. But as Corrine had been halfway through making it, Yuri had come rushing in with Claudia, yelling that she was going into labor. Corrine had hurried to attend to her, and I'd barely managed to wish Claudia good luck before the door closed on me.

That had left me with a half-finished ring. In the end I'd sought out the witch Shayla to help me finish it, and she'd also helped me with the whole sauna setup... including the fluffy white bath robe.

After I'd proposed to River and seen that she was thrilled with the idea of a wedding in The Hearthlands, we didn't spend much longer in the sauna. We had to start getting ready. I carried her down the mountain where we parted ways. She returned to her family, while I returned to my parents to inform them of River's enthusiasm.

Then I had to figure out what clothing I needed to take with me while my parents busied themselves with other arrangements. Shayla knocked on my door, saying she'd been sent by my mom to take my measurements for a custom tuxedo. Apparently she'd already been to see River about a dress.

After Shayla left, I just had to pack a few casual clothes and toiletries. Then my parents returned, accompanied by River, who was carrying a bulging backpack. They informed me that the dragons wanted to leave already.

We headed for the Port, where a large crowd had gathered of countless friends and well-wishers. Even Lucas was among them… and Jeramiah, whom I was not quite so thrilled to see. Brett and Bella were notably absent, though I could hardly blame them for not wanting to attend a wedding with dragons present.

It warmed my heart to see Vivienne standing next to Xavier, holding a smiling baby Victoria. My cousin looked adorable in a pale pink dress and a sunhat. My eyes traveled to Kiev and Mona, who were standing near Erik, Abby, Eli and Shayla. As I caught Kiev's eye, he looked at me apologetically. I guessed he'd heard the latest of my escapades from my parents.

The dragons were already in their beastly forms and there were about twenty-five of them altogether. It was easy to spot those who were getting married since they carried their maidens on their backs. My grandfather and Kailyn located me in the crowd. They rushed toward me, my grandfather pulling me into a strong hug. It felt like I hadn't seen him for ages. The last time had been just after Kailyn's death. He'd looked half dead with distress. But now, with Kailyn by his side again, he looked like the happiest man in the world... almost as happy as me.

All the other wedding attendees would be transported to The Hearthlands by the witches' magic, but since I spotted more than one dragon with nobody on their back, I suggested to River that we fly there instead. How many couples could say they'd traveled to their wedding location on the back of a dragon?

We climbed aboard Ridan, who apparently hadn't had as much luck with the ladies as his fellow shifters. Then all of us left The Shade to embark on the journey. The others vanished along with the witches, while the dragons headed to a small deserted island not far away from us, where a portal led to the realm of the ogres. Reaching the other side of the portal, we launched into the sky and soared over a sparkling ocean. Excitement bubbled up in me as we finally caught sight of another land mass.

"The Hearthlands," Ridan announced cheerily.

Reaching the end of the water, we soared over a world of rolling hills, lush valleys and glittering rivers. It appeared to be summertime here, the trees and flowers in full bloom. We continued to fly, and soon I spotted signs of civilization. A magnificent castle loomed in the distance, a sprawling city built around it. We descended in a cobblestone square right at the foot of the castle. The buildings surrounding us appeared newly erected, their stone walls bright and polished. The square offshot into charming streets lined with an array of boutiques selling everything from garments to instruments. Dragon residents milled around us in their humanoid forms and began to cheer.

"Jeriad!"

"You're back! And with such fair maidens!"

Our dragons greeted their compatriots warmly.

"So much has happened here since you left!" a particularly chirpy man who possessed only one eye exclaimed. "There have been battles and victories, kings lost and found. King Theon has been crowned, and he has a queen!"

I slid off Ridan's back with River as they continued

talking.

"Have you received other arrivals, Charis?" Jeriad asked.

Charis. The name rang a bell. He had been the first dragon to ever visit The Shade. Caleb had speared him in the eye when he'd threatened to burn our island down.

"Other arrivals?" Charis asked.

"We expected there to be a group of citizens from The Shade arriving here. Witches, vampires, even some werewolves…"

"We have seen nothing of the sort yet."

I tensed, looking at River. They should've arrived here way before us, traveling by the witches' magic. I wondered if they'd gotten lost.

"If you like I can fly you around and see if we can spot them anywhere," Ridan offered. "They might have arrived in The Hearthlands but not have known where to find the castle."

"Thanks," I said. "That would be good."

We left with Ridan, while the others entered the castle, apparently going to greet The Hearthlands' new king and queen.

***

We managed to find them after several hours of searching. Truth be told, I didn't mind in the slightest that it took us so long to locate them. River and I enjoyed the ride immensely; it afforded us a greater opportunity to take in this breathtaking realm.

The spell of shadow the witches had cast over the crowd was what helped us spot them. They were roaming around a hillock, looking quite lost. Clearly none of the witches knew The Hearthlands well. Rose was with them, but I didn't think she'd ever been taken as far as the castle and city during her brief visit. She'd spoken of hills and valleys and caves, but not of buildings.

We soared down and they looked relieved to see us. From here, we were able to show them the right direction and soon we were all back outside the castle. The square was empty now, as if everybody had rushed inside with the others to hear the full story of what had happened to their comrades.

We entered the castle with Ridan, emerging in a grand entrance room. A carpet in tones of brown, burgundy and gold lined the floor and shields of iron and gold hung from the walls.

"They will likely be in the royal court now," Ridan announced.

He stopped outside a pair of heavy oaken doors and pushed them open. We emerged in a vast hall whose walls were draped with red-and-orange velvet tapestries. Black stone chandeliers hung from the high ceiling, and in the center was a raised platform upon which were two thrones, occupied by a beast of a man who could only be Theon, and a striking pale-skinned girl with coal-black hair, whom I could only assume was his new queen. The court was packed to the max with dragons.

"Welcome," Theon boomed as he laid eyes on us entering with Ridan. He and his queen left their thrones and descended toward us.

I looked to my sister, who stood next to Caleb holding his hand. She, of all of us, had a special connection with these dragons. Theon had once wished to pursue her as his own.

The king was beaming as he approached, bowing low before my parents and shaking their hands warmly. "Finally," he said, "we have a chance to accommodate you in our own land. Jeriad tells me that you bring three other couples who wish to be wed in dragon country, your son and his love included among them."

"Thank you, Theon," my father replied. "That is correct."

"Since tomorrow marks the end of the week, we have decided that it will be fortuitous to hold the weddings then, rather than wait a few more days for preparation," Theon went on. "Is that agreeable to you?"

My parents looked to me and River. "Yes," River and I responded. Micah, Kira, Matteo and Helina were also in agreement.

"Excellent. Now allow me to introduce you to my wife, Penelope," Theon said, his eyes glinting with pride as he rested his hand on the small of Penelope's back.

Penelope smiled graciously and shook my parents' hands.

"A pleasure to meet you," she said, her gray eyes darting to each of us. "Feel free to call me Nell." She had an American accent. That meant Theon had traveled to somewhere in America to find his soulmate... I couldn't help but wonder how all that had played out. She didn't look older than twenty.

"Your arrival is of impeccable timing," Theon went on. "We have just completed rebuilding the city."

"What happened to your city?" my mother asked.

Theon exchanged glances with Nell before letting out a hearty chuckle. "Let us not speak of the past. At an auspicious time like this, we must look only to the future." His broad smile was contagious.

"You must be tired after your journey," Nell said. "We should arrange for your quarters and some refreshments. Please, come with us."

I was surprised that the king and queen themselves led us out of the court and up a broad set of carpeted stone steps. I looked down at River to see her gazing around the ornate castle in wonderment. I took a moment to remind myself that she was still relatively new to all of this... supernatural craziness. She'd been plucked from the most mundane life possible, had her world turned upside down and been thrust into this whirlwind, whereas I had been acquainted with supernaturals since birth. I couldn't help but admire how she handled herself.

"It's beautiful, isn't it?" I said softly, drawing her eyes to me.

"Yeah," she said, quite breathless. I squeezed her hand and leaned down to kiss her cool cheek.

We arrived in a residential area of the castle and roamed down a long corridor lined with dozens of doors. Theon explained that the apartments on either end would be reserved for the betrothed couples exclusively, with the men sleeping on one side and the women on the other, while all the guests could occupy whichever apartments they liked in the middle.

"We'll bring refreshments shortly," Nell said. "In the meantime, do make yourselves at home."

With that, everyone began milling about the corridor and choosing their apartments.

Rose left Caleb's side and moved to River, taking her hand. "Why don't we share an apartment tonight? Caleb's a big boy. He can manage for one night without me." She winked at her husband, who chuckled.

"I'd love that," River said, grinning.

River and I shared a kiss before the two girls drifted into one of the apartments to my left. That left Caleb and me alone. We exchanged a smirk before moving to the opposite end of the corridor. I chose the door at the very end, which was still unoccupied, while he entered the apartment next door.

When I stepped inside, the suite was extravagant and luxurious, its interior design reminding me of a rustic five-star hotel. The bathroom contained a shower and what looked like a jacuzzi, while the spacious bedroom was dominated by a stately queen-sized bed, draped in deep orange satin and velveteen burgundy cushions. The ceiling above the bed consisted entirely of glass, allowing sun to stream through and affording a view of the breathtakingly blue sky. I could only imagine how stunning this room would be when the stars were out.

Planting down my backpack on an antique wooden table, I sat down on the edge of the bed. A manservant arrived at the door soon afterwards, carrying a silver tray containing a jug of some kind of exotic juice and a basket of peach cupcakes laced with saffron icing.

"A full dinner shall be served later," the man informed me before bowing out of the room.

The cupcakes were divine, so soft and moist they practically melted on my tongue. I ended up finishing the whole lot. The juice was pleasant too, though a little sweet for my taste.

After eating, I left the bedroom to take a shower when there was another knock at my door. I went to open it and found my asshole cousin, Jeramiah, standing on my doorstep.

He looked at me awkwardly. "I'm sorry to disturb you. Could I have a minute?"

"Uh, yeah." I pulled the door open, allowing him to step inside.

He coughed his throat clear, then hung his head. "I've come to apologize."

I clenched my jaw. "It's probably my parents you should be apologizing to."

"I have already."

I paused, eyeing him. It was hard to believe that this apparently guilt-ridden man was the same man I'd known in The Oasis, the leader who was feared and respected by everyone in his coven. He'd been quite an enigma to me at the time.

I thought back to the first time we'd met, back in the hunters' base in Chile. If it hadn't been for him, my story might have ended back there. I never would've escaped. Although he'd had ulterior motives for inviting me to The Oasis, and as horrible and uncertain as that time had been when I'd realized I was trapped there, it'd been a much-needed shelter for me at the time. And it had allowed me to drink blood without needing to kill for it.

His attempt to murder my parents and grandfather was inexcusable in my mind... but I also could not erase his former actions. I was not as forgiving as my mother was—I was still my father's son, after all—but I did not like holding grudges either. Especially when a person appeared genuinely apologetic.

"Then," I began, "if you have gained my family's forgiveness, I suppose you have mine."

Moving up to him, I extended my hand. He took it and shook it firmly.

"Well," he said, stepping back. "I won't take up any more of your time. I'm sure you have ample preparations to be getting on with for tomorrow."

With that, he turned on his heel and let himself out of my apartment.

As I made my way to the bathroom and got in the shower, I was left to ponder over the power of a simple apology. A taming of one's ego, an admission of being fallible... the effect that these things could have on a relationship was profound. I couldn't help but feel that if more people were ready to apologize in the world, it would be a brighter, happier place.

RIVER

The apartment Rose and I stepped into was dreamy. It was just how I imagined a suite in a castle should look like. Beautiful furniture, thick embroidered carpets, dusty tomes lining mahogany shelves, an enormous bed you just wanted to sink into … there was even an old grandfather clock. Rose and I wandered around in a daze, looking through the rooms, and then sat down on the bed. We caught each other's eye and smiled. I still didn't know Rose all that well, despite her being Ben's sister. So much craziness had gone on recently, we'd barely gotten the chance to spend any quality time together. But it was something that I hoped would change in the coming weeks and months.

She reminded me of Ben in some of the things she said, the occasional turn of phrase. Her eye color was also identical to his, as was her dark hair. And she was tall, quite a bit taller than me.

"How are you feeling?" she asked.

"I'm soaring," I replied honestly.

She chuckled. "That's exactly how I felt before my wedding."

There was a knock at the door. I went to open it to find my mother standing in the doorway, along with my two sisters. They had been housed in an apartment just a couple of doors away.

"Can we hang out with you?" Lalia asked.

"Of course," I said, letting them all in.

My mom's smile looked like it had been tattooed on her face. She hadn't stopped grinning since I'd told her I'd accepted Ben's proposal. She pulled me in for a cuddle and kissed my cheek before we entered the bedroom.

I had to return to the door less than a minute later, however, as a group of dragon maids showed up. They all wore the same pretty blue smocks, their hair tied up in buns.

"It's time to begin your skin regimen," they said. "Your bridesmaids can come, too, of course."

Bridesmaids. I realized I hadn't even chosen my bridesmaids yet.

"I wanna be a bridesmaid!" Lalia gushed, zooming out of the door.

"I'll be your bridesmaid," Dafne said.

"And of course I will, too," Rose said, coming to my side.

"Mom?" I grinned at my mother.

"I'll be your matron of honor," she said proudly.

"What about your outfits?" I wondered.

"Don't worry about that," Rose said. "I'll sort it out with Corrine."

The dragons led us down to an atrium of steaming, scented baths down in the lower levels of the castle. Here the maids scrubbed and exfoliated and massaged until my skin felt brand new. As I looked at myself in the mirror afterward, I'd never seen my face so luminous.

We dried and dressed in flowing gowns provided by the maids, then returned to our respective apartments. Since we still had some time before dinner, Rose suggested that we explore the castle a bit.

"Sylvia's in there with Jeriad," Rose said as we roamed the corridor outside, pointing to the door on our left. "It's weird to see so many of my classmates getting married—"

"Hello."

We turned to see Queen Penelope behind us. She had just stepped out of a dragon couple's room, and she was carrying a bouquet of orange roses.

"Hi," I said.

"Thank you for all of this," Rose added. "It's wonderful here."

"You're really very welcome. Theon has spoken to me so highly of all of you." Then she paused. "Are you lost at all? I know how these corridors can be winding..."

"Oh, no," I replied. "We were just wanting to explore a little."

"Would you like me to give you a tour?" she offered.

I exchanged glances with Rose, not wanting to suck up the queen's time. I could only imagine how busy she was. At the same time, a tour sounded amazing.

"We would love that," Rose said. "If you have time."

"I can make time," she said with a grin. She led us away from the corridor and took us on a tour of the entire castle. She showed us the hall of trophies, the vast library, the treasury, even the dungeons. All the while, she recounted to us the story of how she and Theon had met, which Rose had been particularly curious about.

Her story truly was fascinating. And it was quite a revelation discovering how much I had in common with Penelope. She was just a girl like me. A girl who'd been plucked from the mundane world of humans and dumped into the wacky world of supernaturals... in the process losing her heart to one.

Yet when I looked at her, she almost struck me as a dragon herself... at least, she didn't strike me as a regular teenage girl from DC. She spoke with grace and exuded a regal elegance, as though she were born to be a queen.

After she finished giving a thorough tour, she returned us to our apartment. Kissing each other's cheeks, we parted ways until dinner time. We all gathered in the corridor, which was now crowded with other females and males intermingling. With a leap of my heart, I spotted Ben, standing in one corner, talking to Griffin. I crept up to him from behind and placed my hands over his eyes.

"Guess who?" I whispered.

"Oh... That is a difficult question," he muttered, even as his hands reached down and clamped around my thighs. "River. Definitely River."

I giggled, letting go of his eyes. He turned to face me. "You look... rather sparkly," he said, running a hand through my freshly washed hair.

"You look quite clean, too," I remarked.

"Dinner is about to be served!" a voice boomed over to our left. "Please make your way down to the grand court."

Arms around each other, we headed down to the hall. Long tables now lined it. A feast had already been laid out. I was practically drooling as I sat down at the table with Ben. Theon and Nell sat at the head of our table, and other dragons sat with us too. A lithe man with coal-black hair and piercing gray-blue eyes pulled up a chair next to me, giving Ben and me a pleasant smile.

"Welcome to The Hearthlands," he said, pouring himself a drink. "I suppose it's your first time here."

"It is," I replied.

"And you are a couple to be wed?"

"Yes," Ben said.

"Ah." He winced slightly, before taking a swig from his glass. "My name is Lethe, by the way. Congratulations on finding love."

"Uh, thank you," I said.

"I'm yet to find it," he muttered. There was a melancholy expression on his face as his eyes traveled over each of the guests, particularly the females.

Before Ben or I could say anything more to him, Theon and Nell stood up and called for silence.

"Thank you all for gathering here," Theon said. "This dinner is to celebrate the weddings of many fine men and women whom we wish will share strong and prosperous lives together. Now let us eat, drink and be merry."

Theon and Nell sat down again, and dinner was served. I was shocked to learn that there were fifteen courses to this meal. I thought that I had misheard but I had not. I thought that I would make it through the first three courses, maybe the first five if I really paced myself, but by some mysticism, I was able to try every single one. There was something special about the food; as delicious as it was, nothing felt heavy in my stomach; it felt light, and left me salivating for more. By the end, I was well and truly satisfied. I had no stomachache from overeating, I just felt comfortably full. I truly felt sorry for the vampires among us, being unable to taste even a slight bite of this wondrous food.

Lethe proved to be chatty throughout the meal. He seemed to be quite a pleasant soul, asking me things about The Shade, the human realm and particularly about romance and love—which I found rather sweet. In the end I suggested that he come to visit The Shade, if he had no luck finding a female here in The Hearthlands. To my surprise, he seemed delighted by the idea. "Maybe I will," he said.

After we all finished eating, we stood up and bade each other good night before heading for the exit. As we arrived back in our corridor, I stood on my tiptoes and kissed Ben good night. Then Rose and I retreated to our apartment.

After brushing our teeth, we changed into the silk pajamas the dragons had laid out for us, then slid into bed. We chatted for a while—Rose was telling me how she'd managed to speak to Charis and apologize to him—before we both thought it wise to get an early night and switch off the lights.

But I still lay awake long after Rose drifted off to sleep.

Tomorrow.

Tomorrow I will be Mrs. River Novak.

RIVER

Rose did not look surprised the next morning when I told her I'd barely gotten a wink of sleep that night. She just smiled and said, "You really shouldn't have expected to."

People began knocking at our apartment early. First Corrine, arriving with the finished dress to check that it fit right in case she needed to make some last-minute adjustments. As I slipped on the white dress and looked at myself in the mirror, I truly did feel like a princess. It had a heart-shaped neckline and clung to me in just the right places, augmenting the curve of my waist and hips before thinning toward my legs.

"Sheer elegance," Rose said, admiring me.

"Thank you, Corrine," I said breathlessly. "It's more beautiful than I ever thought it would be."

Corrine smiled before saying, "Now, I suggest you take a shower."

I did as she suggested, and by the time I was finished, the dragon maids had arrived. First they massaged moisturising ointments into my skin until I was practically glowing. Then, after I slipped on the dress, they began to do my hair and makeup. The makeup was unlike any I'd ever seen; kept in ceramic pots, it appeared to be made from all-natural materials, and yet it looked more natural and flattering on application than any expensive makeup brand you'd buy in stores. It perfectly complemented my face and looked almost a part of it, rather than painted on.

Then Sofia arrived, carrying a bouquet of roses and a bunch of fuchsia cherry blossoms. Sofia and my mom wove the blossoms into my hair while keeping the bouquet aside. I'd never thought that I could look so beautiful. I could hardly wait for Ben to see me.

Rose and my family changed into their own outfits, and soon Jamil was knocking on the door to inform us that it was time. He looked dashing in a dark gray suit, which I guessed had been provided by the dragons.

As Sofia and my mother bustled me out of the room, I was already picturing myself walking down the aisle. I felt a twinge as I thought of my father, who should have been here to give me away to Ben. He almost seemed like part of another life. I wasn't even sure exactly where he was right now. Still locked up in some Texan jail—that was if he was even still alive. I had drifted apart from my father ever since he'd left my mother, but now, it truly felt like we inhabited separate universes.

I looked up at my brother and looped my arm through his.

"Will you walk me down the aisle?" I asked him.

He looked down at me and smiled. "Of course, sis."

Kira and Helina were also in the corridor looking gorgeous, along with the dragons' brides. We all looked excitedly at one another as we made our way down to the royal court. A number of maids were waiting for us outside the court entrance and they greeted us with smiles.

"The grooms await you inside," one of them said. "You can take it in turns to walk down the aisle. It's up to you who goes first and last."

Hanging back with Jamil, I decided I wanted to go last. The doors opened, and the first bride walked through—Sylvia. Once she had reached Jeriad, the second bride walked through, and so it went on until I was the last girl standing.

My heart pounded. It was my turn to walk through with Jamil. My mother kissed my cheek and whispered good luck while Sofia gave me a gentle hug, careful not to mess up my outfit. She handed me the bouquet of roses and put down my veil.

Then, with Rose, my sisters and mothers behind us, Jamil and I emerged in the glittering court. All the orange and red decorations had been replaced with white, and flowers were scattered everywhere. A haunting organ played as I walked.

My eyes fell on Ben, standing at the end of the raised platform where the thrones had been, now where all the couples had gathered. Wearing a black tux, he looked so tall and handsome, I felt quite breathless. Reaching the platform, Jamil let me go. I stepped onto it and arrived before Ben, trying to steady my uneven breathing. I gazed through my veil into his deep green eyes.

A dragon priest who introduced himself as Einhen climbed to the platform with us once all the couples had gathered, as did Theon and Nell. They went through an odd ceremony of Theon and Nell "approving our coupling" before retaking their seats in the crowd. Einhen was handed an old, heavy book by a maid as well as a goblet of shimmering golden rings. He walked to each of us, handing them out. Then Einhen opened his book and he began to recite: "You will be one flesh, both human and dragon, werewolf and werewolf, vampire and vampire, fae and half-blood. You cannot wish the other ill, or act against them, for to do so is to act against your own body. When the husband fights, so shall the wife; when the wife labors, so shall the husband. There is no difference between these two anymore. They are one. They are complete. Now, recite your own vows and exchange rings, before we seal this decree with the fusion of lips, never again to part."

The first couple on the other side of the platform, Jeriad and Sylvia, exchanged their heartfelt vows, and then the next. My palms were growing sweaty around my bouquet as it got closer and closer to our turn. Soon Helina and Matteo, who stood next to us, were gazing into each other's eyes and swearing their love, and then it was our turn.

Ben, holding my gaze more steadily than ever, cleared his throat and began in a deep, slightly hoarse voice:

"River, no words can adequately describe what I'm feeling in this moment, but I'll start by saying thank you. Thank you for choosing me. As your husband. As your life partner. As your friend. You committed yourself to me even when you didn't have to. You followed me to places you never should have gone. You were there for me in my darkest hours, even when you didn't realize it. Of everything that I may have done, you are my greatest accomplishment. My greatest pride. I vow to love you, protect you, and dream with you for the rest of my existence."

I had to reach up to brush away a tear. My throat felt so

tight. I took a deep breath, trying to prevent my voice from cracking as I began:

"Ben, you so quickly became such a crucial part of my life. Anything that you might have seen as a sacrifice on my part honestly was no sacrifice at all. I did it because I wanted to, because there was no other way I could think to act. You own a piece of me, now and forever. The barrier of physicality *is* no barrier to us. I promise to respect and adore the man you are, for all time... in whatever form that might be."

Even as I said the words, they felt painfully insufficient. I wasn't sure there was any way I could truly express to Ben what I was feeling inside right now.

We exchanged rings before Einhen exclaimed, "Now, seal your oaths with a kiss!"

Lifting my veil, Ben lowered to me and, taking my waist, he pressed his lips to mine in a soft, tender kiss. A kiss I wished would go on forever. As everything faded into the background, we were lost in a world that only Ben and I inhabited. A world that we would make brighter for each other each and every day.

RIVER

As Ben and I drew apart, each of us smiling from ear to ear, I realized the other brides were already throwing their bouquets.

"You'd better throw it." Ben chuckled.

My back to the crowd, I tossed the flowers over my shoulder. There was a wave of cheers and when I turned around I realized that Lethe had caught it. He looked positively thrilled as he examined the bouquet.

Well, good luck, Lethe...

The band began to play, and we followed the couples off the stage. The chairs were pushed aside to make room for tables, where another grand banquet was being laid out. I didn't think my heart could swell any more with happiness as everyone we loved surrounded us with their congratulations. Aiden and Kailyn came up to us and hugged us both, before Aiden held up Kailyn's hand to show us a silver ring on her finger. It looked as though if he smiled any wider, his mouth would split.

"Oh my God! You two are engaged!" Ben gasped.

"I decided to propose the same hour she returned to me," Aiden replied, wrapping an arm around Kailyn.

"It was about time," Ben said, patting his grandfather on the shoulder.

As we all took our seats, I could barely stomach anything, and neither could Ben. We were hungry for each other and nothing else. Our eyes barely parted throughout the meal.

All the other couples left the table as soon as the meal was over, after bidding everyone good night. Ben and I, however, had far more well-wishers to speak to before we could finally break free.

We left the hall and moved swiftly up the staircase, hand in hand. My heart was racing. I knew what was about to follow. As we reached our corridor, he scooped me up in his arms and carried me to his apartment, through to his gorgeous bedroom. He laid me down on the bed and gazed down at me, a sky of stars shining through the window in the ceiling above him. My dress suddenly felt too tight. My mouth was drying out. This would be my first time. As embarrassed as I was to admit it, I didn't really know much about how it all worked. In a bout of insecurity, I found myself wondering whether this was Ben's first time too. I knew he'd had girlfriends before he met me, but I didn't know the depth of those relationships.

Apparently sensing my tension, he brushed his thumbs against my cheeks. "You're so gorgeous when you blush," he said, his voice husky.

I hadn't realized my cheeks were already so flushed.

Pulling me to sit upright, he sat next to me and placed an arm around me. "There's no hurry," he said softly. "We have all night."

All night.

He moved onto the bed and stood on the mattress, pulling at the blinds to reveal more of the stars through the window, until the entire ceiling above us was the night sky.

Then, stepping off the mattress, he circled it and turned off the main lights, leaving only the bedside lanterns to cast a soft light around us.

Removing his jacket, he leaned back on the headboard and beckoned me to him. As I crawled to him, he spread his legs, creating a place for me to sit between his legs, my back against his chest. His arms wrapped around me, hands resting on my stomach. Silence fell as we both gazed up at the stars.

The way I sat against him was lighting me up, any insecurity I'd initially felt quickly ebbed away. I craned my neck to brush the base of his jaw with my lips.

"Unzip me," I whispered.

His fingers moved readily to the top of my zipper. It was clear he'd just been waiting for me to make the first move.

Shivers ran through me as he bared my back. His hands slid from the base of my neck down my shoulders as he rolled the dress off until it had pooled around me, leaving me in my underwear. Although as I turned to face him, his intense green eyes roaming me, I felt as if I wasn't wearing anything at all.

His hands engulfed my waist. I unbuttoned his shirt and removed it, then worked on his belt and pants. I lost all sense of timing after that. Before I knew it both of us were bare. As we kissed, we moved together, our skin touching, our forms molding. His tongue explored my mouth. I felt intoxicated. He pushed me into the soft mattress, one hand running down the side of my ribs, down the curve of my waist, and then down further still.

His kisses grew more intense, more demanding. Lowering more of his weight against me, I felt his tenseness between my legs.

As I sensed he was seconds from moving deeper, he unclasped his lips from mine. His green eyes hooded and blazing with passion, he whispered, "You're my life, River Novak."

My breath hitched, ripples of pain and pleasure surging through me, as he finally made us one.

BEN

I was so drunk with passion, I could barely see straight. I'd never felt such all-consuming desire. I'd never told her this before, but as I was her first, she was mine. I'd had girlfriends in the past, but none of the relationships had ever been serious enough for us to get past second base.

River was more beautiful than I'd ever seen her now, her long glossy hair in soft curls. And I could behold her in all her beauty. As we made love deep into the night, I only fell further into her, physically and emotionally. I couldn't imagine a life without River in it any more. I couldn't imagine an existence without her. It would be vacant, useless.

As I brought River to her climax, tears of ecstasy spilled

from her eyes as she gasped out my name. Burying my hands in her hair, I pressed my lips firmly against hers as I released my own tension.

We rolled over on the bed, breathless and sodden with sweat… and I felt more alive than I'd ever felt in my life.

Reaching for her still-trembling body, I pulled her flush against me and ran my hands slowly down the length of her back. She looked as lost in my eyes as I was in hers.

I remained caressing her until exhaustion finally stole her away from me. Still, I couldn't take my eyes off her face. I hoped that fae could live a long time, because it felt to me that a hundred lifetimes wouldn't be enough for us.

I sensed that she was getting cold. Detaching myself from her gently, I moved her closer to the centre of the mattress. I took a moment to take in the length of her body, the parts of her that had remained secret and shadowed for so long. Then I reached for the blanket, but as I pulled it up over her legs and was about to cover the rest of her with it, I spotted something on her lower stomach. A mark I could have sworn hadn't been there before. A light scar that ran the width of her abdomen.

I frowned, looking at it more closely. Then I finished putting the blanket over her before sliding beneath it next to her. My hand slipped down to her abdomen, my fingers tracing the scar softly enough that she would not wake up.

How could she have gotten a scar like that? It was a huge scar… a surgical scar. The last time I'd seen her abdomen I guessed would have been the time I'd almost given into my passions back in The Oasis, just hours before I'd sent River back to The Shade with Corrine. She'd definitely had no scar then. We'd been naked in that oasis in The Dunes while waiting for Aisha, but the lower part of her had been hidden from me underwater.

Where else can she have gotten it but the hunters' headquarters? What did they do to her? What could they have taken from her?

Frowning with worry, I looked at her face. *Why didn't you tell me, River?*

She must've known that I would see it eventually. Maybe she had intended to tell me, but hadn't found the right moment. I would ask her about it at the next opportunity.

For now, I stopped touching her scar.

I looked back up at the stars above us. I thought back to everything that had happened since I first left The Shade in one of the subs. Being held hostage in The Oasis, the discovery of the jinn, the defeating of the Elder, becoming a ghost and then managing—eventually— to find my way back again…. It was truly stranger than a fairytale. But without it all, I never would have met River. No matter the hardships, that was enough to make it all worth it. For her,

I would do it all over again. *Even bath time with that hunkri.*

My mind lingered on Hortencia and the "lessons" she had been keen to share with me. Her gems of wisdom she'd said I needed to carry with me into the future… and her request for me to slay those Bloodless. My mind buzzed as I tried to make sense of what kind of future she was alluding to and what role the new breed of hunters would play in all of this.

But even as I pondered the possibilities, I realized I was no longer afraid of the future. What would happen, would happen. And I knew now that even if I lost this body again, life didn't stop after death. I would live on in one way or another.

I never had found out what truly existed beyond death—the "other side", the place where most people who died were purported to pass on to. I'd been trafficked to The Underworld before I had gotten the chance to discover the answer.

But as River woke in the early hours of the morning, and we began to make slow, passionate love all over again, that was a discovery I knew I could put off for a long, long time.

RIVER

Ben was home. I'd never felt so secure, so confident, so at peace with myself and the world around me, as when I was in his arms.

I'd fallen asleep in exhaustion after our first time, but when I woke again, we continued making love until the sun streaked the sky above us. Only then did I sleep again, and so did Ben.

When I woke the second time, it was one pm according to Ben's watch—though I doubted that time applied in the dragon realm. Ben was still asleep. Propping my head up on one elbow, I stared at his face. My gorgeous husband. My best friend. My man. My prince.

My heart leapt as his eyes finally opened, allowing me to admire his face in its full glory.

"Good morning, beautiful," I whispered, beaming down at him.

He smiled back, his eyes glazed over. "You stole my line," he said huskily, before pulling me to him and engulfing me in a cuddle.

We both sat up in bed and gazed around us. I hadn't even realized what a mess we had made of the bed throughout the night. The sheet was half off the mattress, and of the dozen or so pillows that had sat on the bed, only two small ones remained.

Ben grinned impishly. "So," he said, cocking his head. "How was it?"

I bit my lower lip, blood rushing to my cheeks. "How was… um, what exactly?"

He broke out in a chuckle. "Seriously? You're going to make me spell it out? All right. Let's put it another way… Did I… uh, tinker with all the right bells?"

My breath hitched just remembering it. "Oh, you did. It's really no wonder they call you Tinkerbell."

He narrowed his eyes on me. "You will be moaning that name by the time I'm finished with you."

Without warning he lurched forward and grabbed me. Straddling my hips, he began tickling me in all the worst places. My stomach wound up in knots from laugher, I cried out, "No, stop! Please! Mercy! Mercy, Tinkerbell!"

Only after I'd gasped the name did he stop, allowing me to sit up and catch my breath.

Then his eyes dropped to my bare abdomen, the smile on his face fading. I knew what he was looking at.

I'd forgotten all about the scar. I still hadn't told him what had happened to me. I hadn't told anyone, not even my mother. It was still painful to talk about because I did not know exactly what they had done, what they might have put in me or taken from me... or maybe they'd just looked around. It was the uncertainty of it all that made me anxious. And I didn't want to worry Ben. But he had seen it now.

"It's, um..." Still, I hesitated.

The concerned look in Ben's eyes only intensified. "It's what, River?" He was dead serious now.

"When I was in the hunters' headquarters—"

He cursed beneath his breath.

"What?" I asked him.

"Go on," he said.

"Yeah, well when I was there... they did something to me. But I'm not sure what it was. They took me to an operating room and drugged me." My voice shook a little as I relived the trauma. "When I woke up I had the scar, but it didn't hurt. M-Maybe they just examined me."

Ben's jaw clenched. "And have you experienced any pain since? Any symptoms at all that could be considered... unusual?"

I shook my head. "No, thank God. I've noticed nothing out of the ordinary."

His fingertips moved to my scar and lingered there for a few seconds. Then, reaching his hands into my hair, he pressed a firm kiss against my forehead.

"If you haven't experienced any symptoms by now, then I'm guessing they've done nothing that will affect you personally, and that's all that matters to me right now. They might have simply taken a sample from you for experimentation... for one of their future projects. But we should have Corrine examine you when we return to The Shade." He paused, a flash of anger in his eyes. "And if we ever do come across the group of hunters who did this to you, I swear, they will sorely regret it."

***

We ended up staying in The Hearthlands for three more days after the wedding. The dragons took us for more rides outside, showing us the entire land right up to its tip, the Obran peninsula.

I enjoyed spending more time with Rose and getting to know Nell better was a treat too. We got on like a house on fire, the three of us, and we spent much time chatting and going for walks when I wasn't relishing the moments I had with my new husband.

It was truly sad when we had to leave, though Theon and Nell promised to visit The Shade some time soon—a promise that Lethe made to me, too.

Our party traveled back to The Shade—including the newly-wed dragons we'd come with. When we returned, to Ben's and my utter surprise, it was to discover a brand-new penthouse. A gift to us from Derek and Sofia. The witches who had remained behind on the island had built it while we were gone. It was not far from the other treehouses, but it was far enough to give us a sense of privacy. We couldn't see any other homes from any of the windows and instead were surrounded by trees, with a magnificent panoramic view of the island.

With the wedding over, after Ben and I had settled into our new home together, he took me to see Corrine about my scar. She performed a number of examinations—during most of which she'd made me unconscious—and in the end she couldn't find any odd insertions, or signs that the hunters had removed anything major from me. She'd said, however, that it was possible they could have extracted an egg or two. If they had, there was nothing we could do about it. I was just relieved they hadn't damaged me.

Once Corrine let me out of the Sanctuary and Ben and I returned to our penthouse, I felt a burning desire to do something that I probably should've done before now, if I had just had the chance.

My father. I had promised him all those months ago that I would try to visit him. Starting this brand-new chapter of my life with Ben felt like the right time. I expressed my desire to Ben and of course he was supportive. I asked him if he would come with me and he said he would. My mother thought it best that I see what state my father was in before my other siblings visited. My sisters, still being young, could be easily upset, and Jamil's mind was also still fragile in some ways. If my father was okay, we would go to see him together afterward, and then make a much needed visit to my grandfather.

So Ben and I set off together. One of the perks of being married to a fae was that you never needed to rely on any kind of transport. He could fly wherever we needed to much faster than a plane. I knew which prison my father was staying at, and we brought a bunch of maps and navigating equipment.

We met with a few complications along the way—such as getting lost—but eventually we arrived at the Texan jail where my father had been transferred.

Fortunately, the lighting inside was garish, and Ben's

natural aura wasn't too noticeable. I enquired as to whether my father was here, and I was relieved to learn that he was. Indeed, I managed to make an appointment to see him this very day. Back on Rikers Island, I doubted I would have been able to do this. I wondered if his visiting times had been relaxed due to good behavior.

As we moved into the designated meeting area and my father appeared behind the glass, an overwhelming sense of déjà vu washed over me. I hurried to the window, gazing at him through the barrier. He wore the same orange uniform, and his ragged face—far too old for his age—lit up as he took me in. He was blinking as he stared at me, as if he couldn't believe I'd really come. Pain and guilt stabbed me.

"River," he rasped, his hands pressed flat against the glass.

"Dad," I breathed, my voice choked up.

"Darling, how are you? I thought I might never see you again."

Tears brimmed in my eyes. "I'm so sorry, Dad," I gasped. I could barely even bring myself to make an excuse for why I had left it so long. I should've found a way.

"Are you all right?" he asked.

"I-I'm fine," I said, forcing a smile. "Never been better, actually. H-How are you?"

"I'm…" He hesitated, wetting his lower lip tentatively, as though weighing his words. "I'm… doing better, I think," he said. "At least, I think I am. They give me more privileges now. Things that I couldn't do before. You know, extra time outside the cell." He paused again as his eyes fell on Ben. "And who is this?" my father asked curiously. "You brought a friend?"

I reached for Ben's hand, and pulled him closer. "Dad," I said, finally managing to steady my voice, "meet my husband, Ben."

My father's jaw dropped open. "Your... husband?" he gasped. He gaped at me, then narrowed his eyes as if wondering if this was some kind of joke.

"Yes," I said, smiling more broadly. "We got married, like, a week ago."

"Oh," he breathed, gazing at Ben in wonderment. I wondered if he had noticed a strange aura around Ben, or if he was just sizing him up. "It's nice to meet you," he said, his hand hitting the glass as he moved instinctively to shake Ben's hand. *He can't even shake the hand of his new son-in-law.*

"It's an honor to meet you, Mr. Giovanni," Ben said, moving closer to the glass and placing his own hand against it, where my father's was. Ben couldn't have known how much that small gesture meant to me.

"H-How did you meet?" my father asked, still looking in a daze.

"Oh… we, uh…" I began to stammer. I really hadn't been prepared for that question, just as my father *really* wouldn't be prepared for the answer.

"In a sauna," Ben answered for me smoothly.

I grinned at Ben in appreciation. *Brilliant.*

After that, my father asked some more questions about Ben—what his interests were, what he did for a living, and other such things—which Ben just as deftly answered without actually lying. Then, after my father asked after my mother and siblings, our time with him was drawing to a close.

When the guard called to him, urgency filled my father's eyes. "I love you, River. My strong, beautiful girl. I need you to know that I'm proud of you. Please, don't ever forget that… And I-I hope that I can see you again. Sooner, than last time. You know, I really think that if I manage to keep up my behavior, I might be let out earlier."

I smiled faintly. "I promise I'll come back sooner. And remember that I love you, too, Dad." Then the guard took him away.

My father's last words lingered in my mind, long after the door had closed. They reminded me all too much of the hopes he'd used to instill in us before dashing them to the ground. I'd heard words like those too many times before to take them seriously. *Maybe he will, maybe he won't.*

Whatever the case, my happiness did not rest upon what he decided to do with his life anymore. And neither did my mother's or siblings.

We had found a new life. A home. Happiness.

We had found The Shade.

And I... I had found Ben.

DEREK

It took a while for Sofia and me to come down from cloud nine after our son's wedding. It had been not only a beautiful experience, but also an intensely nostalgic one—more so for me than Sofia, I suspected. Watching my son look upon his new bride as she walked toward him down the aisle... he reminded me so much of myself. The day I had stood at the end of the aisle, gazing at my beautiful bride, the love of my life, approaching me in her trailing white dress, her auburn hair in curls. I knew exactly how Ben had felt in that moment, and I saw the same look in his eyes. I saw the profound love and affection he held for River, and I sensed in that moment that they would be just as happy together as Sofia and I were.

While we were in dragon country, Lucas had also done as he'd promised. He'd found the time to talk to Sofia—while being sensitive enough to have me present also—and he'd given her as heartfelt an apology as a man could. Sofia had nodded, accepting, and assuring him that if he kept up his good behavior, there was no reason he could not fully earn her forgiveness. I sensed from the look in his eyes that he did not take her words lightly and in the coming weeks, we would see him make amends for a number of grievances he had caused us—I guessed beginning after his promised trip with Jeramiah to visit Jeramiah's mother's tombstone.

On our return to The Shade, before launching into sorting out accommodation for our new group of female jinn, we got to see Claudia's baby for the first time. A baby girl. She shared Claudia's blonde hair as well as her brown eyes, though I was sure that she had Yuri's nose and would likely have his dimples.

"We've named her Claudine," Claudia said to me.

I stared at her. "Are you serious?"

"Mhm."

I glanced at Yuri, whose expression was stoic, then back at Claudia. "How can you pick such a similar name to—?"

"Well, she's my mini-me," Claudia retorted. "What better name for her?"

I looked at Claudia in disbelief. Then, to my relief, a smile

308

cracked her face. "I'm pulling your leg, Derek. You don't think I'm still *that* narcissistic, do you?"

"Her name is Ruby," Yuri chuckled.

"I like that better," I said, letting out a breath. I couldn't deny that for a moment I had actually thought Claudia had reverted to her old self. "A lot better."

Next, we visited the jinn. After much discussion, they ended up choosing to make their quarters in The Black Heights. Although it meant clearing out a number of our grain storage rooms, the grain could easily be stored elsewhere. I actually couldn't have picked a better location, since it was far enough from the witches that they wouldn't step on each other's toes. Dragons and jinn didn't have a problem getting on, so there was no issue with them living in close proximity. The jinn preferred to create their own apartments with their magic once we'd cleared the chambers, so we left them to it.

The three fae, Nolan, Chantel and Marcilla also needed accommodation; we ended up offering them two spare beach houses, near where Mona and Kiev used to live. They were thrilled and thanked me countless times. I suspected that, after their stay in The Underworld, they would have been grateful even if I'd sent them to share Brett's cave.

After attending to a number of other pressing matters that had cropped up during our time away, Sofia and I found ourselves with some time together one evening. As we returned to our apartment, I caught her hand and pulled her into the music room. I seated her on the bench in front of the piano. Sitting next to her, I began to play. Sofia let out a soft sigh and relaxed against me, resting her head against my shoulder.

"I'd almost forgotten how beautifully you play," Sofia murmured.

"Thank you." I grinned.

We lapsed into silence, letting the music engulf us.

Ah, peace at last... Both of our twins safe and married. Our island—with the addition of jinn—now a stronger fortress than ever. And now here I was, alone in a room with Sofia and my music.

There were few places I was happier than in front of a piano. It'd been so long since I'd gotten the chance to touch an instrument.

A wave of nostalgia washed over me as I found myself playing one of my favorite tunes. I realized that it was the same tune that I'd played for Sofia the very first time I had taken her into my music room, all those years ago. She had leaned against me then, as she was doing now, breathing gently with her eyes closed as she listened to me play.

"I love you, Derek Novak," Sofia whispered.

I stopped playing and cupped her face in my hands. I

gazed down into her emerald-green eyes that saw through to my soul, and ran the tip of my nose down the bridge of hers before locking our lips. There was no way I could express how much I loved my wife. My love burned as deep for her as the day I'd made her mine.

"Shall we sleep in our special place tonight?" I suggested with a smile.

She grinned up at me. "Why not?"

As I went to gather our toothbrushes while Sofia packed some towels, I was surprised to hear a knock at the door.

Sofia and I exchanged glances. It was rather late for someone to be disturbing us without good reason...

We both dropped our things and went to the front door. We opened it to see Eli standing there. He had a look of concern on his face.

This had happened too many times in the past year for me to not immediately expect bad news.

"What is it?" I asked.

I was relieved when a small smirk curved his lips. "No need to look at me like I'm the Grim Reaper."

"Well, that's kind of what you've been," I muttered. "I can't think of a single instance when you've shown up at our doorstep after hours with good news."

"Well," Eli said, coughing, "it's not exactly cause for a party, but it's not an emergency either. It's... something to be aware of. It's on a local news station which I don't believe you have here, so you might as well come to mine."

Sofia and I exchanged curious glances before acquiescing.

As the three of us left our treehouse and began running through the redwoods, I had no idea what Eli was about to show us. Just as I had no idea what the future had in store for us. How could I, when, as immortals, our journey through life appeared more winding than the mind of an oracle?

But whatever lay ahead, I could be certain of one thing: this beautiful island that surrounded us. This magnificent haven we were privileged enough to call home. The Shade. One way or another, it would always remain our sanctuary. It had for hundreds of years and it would for the rest of eternity. I knew it from the very core of me.

Because The Shade was a reflection of its people. In its strength. In its tenacity.

And The Shade was true to its inhabitants. As true as the love that burned in their hearts for each other.

WHAT'S NEXT?

Thank you for accompanying me on Ben and River's journey. Their story has held a very special place in my heart, and it's with sadness that I say this has been their final book.

However, although Ben and River's story has ended, The Shade has not!

A new era has dawned for the Novak clan. An era in which The Shade has become such a fortress that threats to the island are no longer possible. They have become protectors; fighters, warriors, every one a hero.

Witness the Novaks in all their strength and in all their glory. In all their love and all their friendship.

Embark on a breathtaking new journey with an exhilarating fresh romance, while reuniting with all your favorite characters and meeting exciting new ones.

A Clan of Novaks is the beginning of a BRAND NEW adventure that will have you swooning, gushing, and clinging to the edge of your seat!

A Clan of Novaks releases April 5th, 2016.

Please visit: www.bellaforrest.net for details.

Here's a preview of the kick-ass cover:

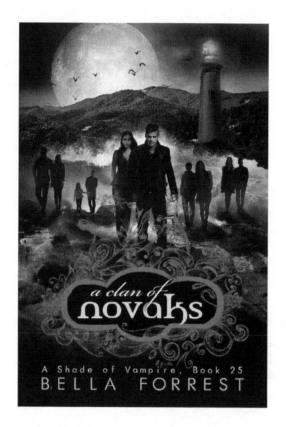

Love,

Bella x

P.S. Join my VIP email list and I'll send you a personal reminder as soon as I have a new book out. Visit here to sign up: www.forrestbooks.com

(You'll also be the first to receive news about movies/TV show as well as other exciting projects coming up!)

P.P.S. Follow The Shade on Instagram and check out some of the beautiful graphics: @ashadeofvampire

You can also come say hi to me on Facebook: www.facebook.com/AShadeOfVampire

And Twitter: @ashadeofvampire